RUDE MECHANICALS

RUDE MECHANICALS

KAGE BAKER

Illustrated by J. K. Potter

SUBTERRANEAN PRESS • 2007

Second Printing

ISBN
978-1-59606-087-6

Subterranean Press
PO Box 190106
Burton, MI 48519

www.subterraneanpress.com

ACKNOWLEDGEMENT

The author would like to thank Mr. Herbert Poetzl, curator of the Reinhardt document collection at Binghamton University. Special and particular thanks are in order to Dr. Carol Merrill-Mirsky, director of the Hollywood Bowl Museum, for her gracious and enthusiastic help in solving the mysteries surrounding Max Reinhardt's nearly-forgotten stage extravaganza.

HOLLYWOOD, 1934

One

Full of vexation come I, with complaint…

Lewis sat alone in his booth at Musso and Frank's, smiling down at a perfect martini. The booth was dark wood, above which there was just enough light to make out the restaurant's mural depicting a forest landscape. In this dim and cozy bower his drink shone out with a silvery light, its icy disk fragrant with aromatic gin, just a polite nod of vermouth.

As he fished out the small olive and popped it in his mouth, Lewis murmured a prayer of thanks to the goddess Athena, bestower of the olive tree on mortals. Lewis generally prayed to Apollo, having been left, as an infant, by the statue of that deity in the temple of Aquae Sulis in 130 A.D; but he liked to give credit where credit was due.

Little beams of light from the swirling gin danced on the table, subsided. All was calm. The universe was a rational and ordered place…

There came a reek of sweat, thinly masked by Burma-Shave Lotion. Lewis lifted his head, frowning, looking about;

a second later he nodded in recognition as another immortal slid into the booth.

"Joseph, what on earth have you been doing?"

The other man sighed, loosening his tie. The two immortals presented a striking contrast to each other. Lewis was slight, fair-haired and immaculately groomed; Joseph was stocky, dark, sloppily shaven and had a coffee-stain on his right cuff. It was displayed as he waved for a waiter. Lewis recoiled from the fresh wave of sweat. "And when did you *bathe* last?"

"Yesterday morning. In the bus station," said Joseph. He noticed Lewis's martini and grabbed for it. Lewis raised it out of reach.

"Get your own! What were you doing in a bus station?"

"Tailing Wallace Beery," said Joseph, in a weary voice. "You don't want to know."

"Ohh." Lewis nodded sympathetically. In his twenty-thousand or so years Joseph had worked as an Egyptian priest, a Roman centurion, a Byzantine spy, a Spanish inquisitor and a number of other difficult occupations, but seldom for so demanding an employer as Louis B. Mayer. "Pancho Villa's on another rampage, is he?"

"Yeah, the son of a bitch. Waiter! Scotch on the rocks. Make it a double."

"It's not easy being a studio dick, I suppose," said Lewis.

"You can say that again," said Joseph, sagging back in the booth. His black eyes were sunk back in his head with exhaustion. "Goddam Hays Code. This week, I jumped through hoops so Gentleman Wally doesn't do five to ten on a manslaughter charge. Last week, I had to dig through Jean Harlow's garbage for a certain letter. The week before that, I was pulling Jack Barrymore out of a brothel in Ensenada at one AM to get him all the way back to a makeup chair in

Culver City by five AM. Don't let anybody ever tell you a Model A can't do eighty-five. We outran five cops between Escondido and Culver City. And Garbo slapped my face. Again."

"'What? And leave show business?'" Lewis quoted, chuckling.

In silence Joseph transmitted: *And on top of everything else, the Company picks now, of all times, to throw me a job.*

Lewis raised his eyebrows. The Company to which Joseph referred was better known, in cyborg circles, as Dr. Zeus Incorporated. Joseph's orders came from an all-powerful cabal of research scientists and investors based in the twenty-fourth century, who had invented time travel and immortality. Having failed to find a way to make these inventions marketable, however, they had used them to create immortal cyborg servants based in the past, who could be used to retrieve precious objects lost in time and send them on to the future, there to command obscenely high prices from private collectors.

What sort of job? Lewis transmitted back.

Well, that was sort of what I wanted to talk to you about. Joseph straightened up and looked at Lewis with wide sincere eyes. *You're working with Max Reinhardt right now, aren't you? The German theater guy?*

Lewis took a fortifying sip of his martini before replying. *I've inveigled myself into a position as one of his assistants. He's producing* A Midsummer Night's Dream *at the Hollywood Bowl.*

Company job, right? What are you after?

Some billionaire up in 2342 wants Reinhardt's notes and promptbook. Why do you ask?

Can you get me a job on the crew?

Lewis, midway through another sip, nearly choked. He set the glass down hastily. "But—Joseph, that's Facilitator work! I'm only a Literature Preservation Specialist," he said aloud, so shocked he was.

"Hey, you're a smart guy. Improvise," said Joseph breezily. He looked up with a smile of gratitude at the waiter who brought his drink. "Thanks a million, pal. How about a menu?"

The waiter obliged in silence. Joseph took a fortifying gulp of Scotch and studied the menu, ignoring Lewis's expression of dismay. "Say, is the chicken pot pie any good?"

"Never mind the chicken pot pie! What could you possibly want with Mr. Reinhardt? He doesn't run in—" Lewis tried to find a tactful way to say it, and couldn't—"your sort of circles. No fisticuffs, no boozing, no gambling. No ladies of the evening. No mob connections."

"This has nothing to do with Reinhardt," said Joseph. "I just need a job on the construction crew. You can get me one, right?"

"Wrong," said Lewis. "Joseph, I'm not even an assistant director, for gods' sake! I'm a director's assistant and translator! I just explain things to Mr. Reinhardt and keep his production notes tidy."

"And I'm sure you do a swell job, too," said Joseph. "I'll bet he's never had such tidy notes in his whole life. Which is why he'll undoubtedly appreciate *your* valuable recommendation that he employ your dear friend who's the best set painter in Hollywood."

"But you aren't," said Lewis. "And anyway, there aren't any painters on this show. It's outdoors. He's even having the Bowl shell taken off. We're putting in trees instead. Moss and cobwebs and things. And a giant ramp for a procession onstage."

"Well, O.K., so I'm the best giant ramp builder in Hollywood."

"But you aren't!"

"I built goddam pyramids in Egypt, I can build a ramp at the Hollywood Bowl," said Joseph, exasperated. "For crying out loud, Lewis, use your imagination! *This is a Company job.* And what All-Seeing Zeus wants, he gets. Don't make me go to your case officer on this."

"You would, too, wouldn't you?" said Lewis waspishly. He drained his martini at a gulp. "Why don't you just use your awesome powers of persuasion on Mr. Reinhardt yourself? He's sitting right over there."

"No kidding?" Joseph leaned out of the booth to stare.

"*Discreetly*, for heaven's sake! He doesn't like being bothered," said Lewis. Joseph leaned back again but kept his gaze on the occupant of the table across the room. He saw a middle-aged man with stern heavy features and blazing blue eyes. Max Reinhardt looked like a Beethoven symphony personified, all thunder and lightning, but at the moment he was placidly dawdling over the remains of a substantial dinner.

"Talk about lucky coincidences," said Joseph. He got to his feet, shot his cuffs, straightened his tie, and approached Reinhardt's table with his hand out and an ingratiating smile on his face.

"You'll be sorry," Lewis murmured, but was ignored.

"Say, Mr. Reinhardt, what a pleasure to run into you like this!" said Joseph, in his most captivating tones. "Joseph Denham. May I trouble you for a moment of your time?"

The great man looked up, disconcerted. "I beg your pardon?" he said, in German.

"I just wanted to say, Mr. Reinhardt, how happy we are to have you here in Hollywood, bringing your unique brand of showmanship to our shores," said Joseph, switching to perfectly-accented Viennese with overtones of Berlin. He shook Reinhardt's hand. "And I just wondered whether you might have an opening in your show for a man of my talents.

Maybe I should explain—"

"Please," said Reinhardt, with a shy smile that did not extend to his eyes. "I—er—" he fumbled in his coat. "One moment please—I have a card case." Further fumbling did not produce one. He glanced down at the remnants of his meal and said, "Would you have the kindness to excuse me one moment?"

"Of course!" Joseph stepped back. "Take all the time you want."

Reinhardt walked to the back of the restaurant and vanished around the corner of a booth. Five minutes passed. Ten more went after them.

"I ordered you the chicken pot pie," Lewis called. "You may as well come back, you know. He's halfway to his hotel by this time."

"No, he isn't," said Joseph, though with a sinking feeling. "I think he's looking for his card case. Maybe he dropped it in the john."

"Yes, of course," said Lewis. Joseph waited five more minutes and then returned to the booth, sighing.

"Hell. He took a powder, didn't he?"

"It's just possible," said Lewis, without a trace of sarcasm. "That's not the way to approach him, you know. Reinhardt can vanish in a puff of smoke when he's feeling pressured. Doesn't quite inhabit the same base terrestrial regions as you or I. He's a true artist. And you just might have given the impression you were a Nazi spy, with that accent. He's a Jewish refugee, in case you were unaware."

"But I used his own accent. Mortals like that. It relaxes them," said Joseph.

"I use British-accented schoolbook German," said Lewis. "It's what he expects. I'm afraid you came off a bit unnecessarily Mephisthophelean."

"How are you going to get me on the crew, then?"

Lewis pursed his lips. "Let's just pretend for a moment that our masters did me the honor of programming me as a big-cheese Facilitator, like you, instead of as a humble Preserver. Of course I'll wave my magic wand and get you a job on the show, Joseph; nothing easier! Perhaps you ought to tell me why you need one."

"It's a long story." Joseph slumped over his drink. "You ever hear of the Lost Treasure of the Cahuenga Pass?"

"I beg your pardon?"

"I guess not, huh?"

"No," said Lewis. "No, I haven't. This is just going to get weirder, isn't it?"

"1865," said Joseph. "Maximilian ruling Mexico, as much as he was able. The rebellion happens. Mazatlan, big wealthy port city with a lot of European émigrés living there, declares for the rebels. But the rebels are running out of guns and ammo. Freedom-loving Mexicans pass the hat to raise money to buy more. Rich mortals donate gold and jewels.

"The treasure's sent north by ship, with two Mexican captains and a couple of English mercenaries who just happen to be there agitating against French rule. Imagine that, huh? The plan is to take the loot to San Francisco, buy arms with it and take them back to the heroic freedom fighters. But, en route, the Mexican who knew all the contacts dies, without getting the chance to pass the secret names to his fellow conspirators.

"So the three remaining mortals land in San Francisco with all this fairly heavy and obvious treasure. They don't know who they can trust. They decide to ride out into the hills and bury the treasure, then go back to Mazatlan to find out who they're supposed to contact. They do. They come back to San Francisco, but the treasure's gone. Doesn't make any difference in the long run; Maximilian goes down anyway, poor dope.

"One of the English guys passes the story of the treasure on in his family, and one of his descendants is one of the founders of Dr. Zeus. Or something like that. Anyway, the treasure got the Company's attention."

"Cahuenga Pass is a long way from San Francisco, Joseph," said Lewis, taking another sip of his martini.

"I'm coming to that, O.K.? What happens is, this shepherd is grazing his flocks in the hills above San Bruno and he sees the three guys burying the treasure. As soon as they go, he digs it up again.

"Then he loads it on two mules and a horse and decides to make tracks. He goes south and gets as far as…"

"The Cahuenga Pass," said Lewis, pointing over Joseph's shoulder in the direction of the Pass.

"Yeah. Where his nerve gives out. He stops at a stage-coach inn and tavern. Guess who runs it?" ·

"No idea," said Lewis. Then he winced. "Oh—wait—that was where—"

At that moment the waiter brought his veal cutlet and Joseph's chicken pot pie, and there was appreciative silence for a while before Joseph resumed, speaking through a full mouth:

"Stagecoach inn's a Company HQ. The mortal brings the loot straight to the arms of Dr. Zeus, can you beat it? The operative running the place is a Security Tech. He reports straight to the Company and is told to persuade the mortal that Los Angeles is really dangerous (which it was) and he really ought to hide anything valuable he might happen to be carrying nearby and rest up a while.

"Which the mortal obligingly does. He goes up into what's now the Hollywood Bowl and buries the loot in six little caches around an ash tree. Goes back to the tavern and gets drunk. Keeps drinking. Drinks some more. The Security Tech sneaks out, finds where the loot is buried, contacts Dr. Zeus for further orders. Company tells him to leave it be, but make sure no mortals get a chance to get near it.

"So the Company op takes a subsonic generator up there, one of the old field models, and hides it in a bush by the ash tree and switches it on. It puts out its fourteen-cycle note at maybe sixty decibels, so any mortals coming close will panic if they walk into its range.

"Meanwhile, back at the tavern, the shepherd drinks himself into collapse. He has a local friend who comes and moves him to his house, so he can recover there. Only he doesn't. He gets worse and dies. But before he does—he tells his friend about the treasure, and where he buried it."

"And his friend goes to dig it up, but runs into the subsonic field and panics?" said Lewis.

"Has an anxiety attack so bad he has a stroke and dies," said Joseph. "Though not before the story gets out. *Madre de Dios, it's a Cursed Treasure!* So none of the local mortals ever dare come search for it again. And there it sits, until the 1880s. This was where I came in."

"Wait. The treasure's hidden in the Hollywood Bowl. You need to dig it up?" Lewis knit his brows. "But you could go up there anytime, Joseph. You needn't be employed there. The place is completely open."

"No, I don't need to dig it up. There's a complication," said Joseph. He held up his empty glass and waved it hopefully in the direction of a waiter. The waiter glided close, took the empty glass and returned a moment later with a full one.

"There would be a complication," said Lewis.

"1885," said Joseph. "First big real estate boom in L.A. County. The joint is filling up with mortals. Company decides the treasure needs to be moved to a place it'll stay hidden. I get orders to go to the Cahuenga Pass HQ. I report for duty and it's Palinurus in command there now, remember him? He sets me up with a cover as a Basque shepherd.

"So I go back in there and dig up the treasure, move the rest of it to a different location close by. One that'll have a famous landmark close to it pretty soon that's going to stay there for the rest of recorded history, so the Company *knows* it's going to be pretty much undisturbed. With a couple of brief exceptions."

"Oh," said Lewis. "Light dawneth."

"It doth, huh?" Joseph drained his drink and crunched ice.

"Why didn't the Company just have you retrieve the whole treasure right then?"

"It'd contradict the Temporal Concordance. More than that, you don't need to know."

"Oh."

"Anyway, I go back to HQ. Palinurus and I spread the word that some coins and jewelry have been found, up in that canyon. The local mortals remember the story from twenty years before and everyone tells me, *Senor, be careful, that's a Cursed Treasure!* And I say *Ha! Don't be foolish, there's no such thing as a curse!* Then I leave, announcing I'm going home to my native Pyrenees, and six months later Palinurus spreads the word: *That Basque fell overboard on his way home and drowned! And what sunk him was...the Cursed Treasure, sewn into his coat!*"

"Unnecessarily theatrical, if you ask me," said Lewis.

"Yeah, well, it kept the mortals from snooping around up there," said Joseph. "And now the Company sends word it would like a Company op on the spot to make sure Mr. Reinhardt's stupendous colossal earthworks don't disturb a

Company cache. That's where I come in. All *you* have to do is get me on the work crew."

"I'll do my best," said Lewis. "I have my hands full with my own mission, though, I warn you. I won't be able to help you much."

Joseph grinned. "Relax! How many centuries of experience have I racked up, misdirecting mortals on account of Dr. Zeus didn't want them to see something? *'I will lead them up and down'*!"

"Fair enough. I may be able to get Mr. Girton to take you on. You won't bother Mr. Reinhardt again, though, will you?" said Lewis. "I don't think you made a favorable impression on him, somehow."

"Trust me!" said Joseph cheerily, and signaled the waiter for another drink.

TWO

So quick bright things come to confusion...

Joseph was as good as his word, though Lewis (hurrying along in Reinhardt's wake clutching sketch pads and the promptbook) spotted him on the work crew a scant week later.

Joseph had taken some pains with his disguise as a mortal laborer, purchasing overalls, workboots and a battered felt hat from an old-clothes dealer. When he spotted Lewis, he lifted his hat with an ironical smile. Reinhardt didn't seem to recognize him, at least; but on those occasions when the great man floated through the set, his eyes seemed focused on the faery forest that didn't yet exist, rather than the acoustic shell that was in the process of being moved from its base by a horde of sweating workmen.

Sunlight poured down into the Bowl valley, soft and with a certain heaviness; it was easy to imagine the light falling like a blanket, muffling the noise of the crowbars and chains. Any time work stopped, a dreamlike silence descended. The immense half-cup of the shell inched its way along, surreal as a pyramid walking under timeless light, and finally vanished like a magician's trick.

Truckloads of earth were brought in, then, mountains of loam, to be shoveled and sculpted on the wide bare stage; then the base was built for the great trestle that was to bridge the ravine behind the stage. Reinhardt stalked out across the valley floor to watch, mopping his face with a handkerchief in the heat, barely noticing Lewis at his elbow. He frowned at the timber framework against the bright sky. Lewis squinted up at it hoping Reinhardt hadn't noticed Joseph, swaggering with a bucket of nails along an eight-inch cat-walk three stories above.

"*Es geschieht schnell, Herr Professor,*" said Lewis.

"Yes, but," said Reinhardt. He fell silent a moment, apparently forgetting Lewis was there. At last he scowled and waved his hand at the raw planks and beams. "Too *real,*" he said, as though to himself. "It must be clouds and moonlight. Herr Thomas must build mist, and stars. Book—?…"

Hastily Lewis put the promptbook and a pencil in Reinhardt's hand. Reinhardt opened it, licked the end of the pencil and set to scribbling in a margin. He walked away, failing to look where he was going, and Lewis had to steer him around three ladders and a lumber pile before they got back to the stage. Behind them, Lewis heard Joseph whistling the *St. Louis Blues.*

The way was cleared at last for the Wood Near Athens to rise.

Lewis followed like a shadow as Reinhardt stalked through the forests of Calabasas, hand-selecting live trees to be planted on the stage. No mere spindly little ornamentals, either; gigantic oaks, elms and aspen trees were dug up, loaded onto wagons and trucked into the Bowl. There Reinhardt sat at the top of the house like God with a megaphone, directing as each tree was moved into precisely the right spot. A few feet this way—a few feet that way—more forest, more shadows, more mystery!

Watching him, Lewis shook his head in sympathy. It would never be exactly as Reinhardt dreamed; nothing could. *How lucky mortals are,* thought Lewis, *that they never live long enough to learn it.*

LEWIS!!!!!

Lewis sat bolt upright in bed, convinced the telephone was ringing. It wasn't. A mortal might have looked next at his alarm clock, but Lewis did not require one. He stared around at his apartment, noting the predawn gloom beyond the windows. No desperate cyborg clinging to the fifth-story ledge; no one standing by his worktable, where his inks and papers were tidily arranged around the copies he was making of Reinhardt's papers. Tea makings laid out in the kitchenette, his solitary three-minute egg and slice of toast still inhabiting the realm of yet-to-be, his carefully-pressed suit still over the chair where he had laid it out the night before. He was, as usual, alone. So who—

Lewis, where the heck are you?

Lewis scowled and pressed his fingertips to his temples. *You needn't transmit at that volume! And I'm in bed, where do you think? It's half-past-six.*

O.K., sorry. I've been signaling for five minutes. Some people have to get up early, you know? Joseph seemed to be struggling with his temper. *Look, I'm in a jam. Some goddam mortal wrecked my car. I need a lift to the Bowl. I'm late for work.*

Crumbs. I'm still in my pajamas. I'll be there as soon as I can. You're over on Morningside Court, aren't you?

Just throw on a bathrobe!

I can't walk through the lobby in my dressing gown! Why can't you take a streetcar?

It'll take too long. Come on, Lewis, be a pal!

Muttering to himself, Lewis scrambled out of bed and got dressed. It was ten minutes before he retrieved his Plymouth coupe from the Orchid Apartments garage, and drove straight into morning rush hour traffic. There was a traffic accident at Highland; he lost more time casting about for Joseph's street. Altogether it was a full hour before he spotted Joseph, pacing back and forth on the sidewalk in front of a tiny apartment court and shouting at a cop who stood beside Joseph's Ford, which was now fenderless and doorless on its left side and displaying more of its under-carriage than was strictly proper.

"No, it was parked!" he was saying. "I'm up at five, I'm shaving, I hear this helluva crash, I go running out in my un-derwear and see this huge Oldsmobile backing out of my car with some idiot college kid at the wheel! He took off toward Vine! What are you going to do about it? *There* you are!" He turned to Lewis. "What kept you?"

He went to pull open the door of Lewis' car, but the cop put a hand on his shoulder.

"I'll tell you what I'm going to do about it, bub—I'm going to take an accident report while you cool down. Or would you like to go downtown?"

"He doesn't," said Lewis. "Joseph, talk to the nice po-liceman."

Joseph talked to the nice policeman for another twenty minutes, during which time a neighbor emerged from one of the other cottages in the court, inspected the damage, and offered to tow Joseph's car to his machine shop and do a re-pair estimate. It was eight-thirty by the time Lewis was able to pull away from the curb again, with Joseph fuming in the seat beside him.

"How the hell could you get *lost?*" Joseph demanded. "You're a cyborg."

"It might interest you to know that we're programmed with map coordinates taken in 1960," said Lewis. "It just so happens your address isn't on those maps. The whole block will be bulldozed for parking lots, as I discovered when I did an emergency access of the 1926 Sanborn survey, by which point I'd been around the block at Sunset and Vine six times."

"You...oh. Well, crap. What stupid data entry tech didn't catch that?" Joseph gnashed his teeth. He subsided and glared out the window. "You'd still have gotten there faster if you hadn't shaved before you left."

"I haven't shaved," said Lewis, with a certain edge in his voice.

"Really?" Joseph turned to peer at him. "Well, some guys have all the luck." He turned back and made an impatient gesture at a milk truck that had just pulled out in front of them. "Look at this! Where's he think he is, a dance floor? Jeez, if I'd gone ahead and taken the streetcar, I'd have been there by now. Son of a bitch. Serves me right. You know, I should have been warned about this! How come that cop's accident report doesn't make it into the Temporal Concordance? What are those guys up in 2334 *doing*, anyway, huh?"

"Failing to plot Event Shadows," said Lewis.

"You're telling me. Sometimes it *stinks*, being a cyborg!"

Lewis dropped him off in front of the Bowl with a sense of relief, and went home to shave.

><

Reinhardt was in a fine mood that morning, scarcely noticing when Lewis showed up late. He flung out his arm at the Wood Near Athens, his blue eyes shining.

"*Wunderbar,*" he said.

"Yes, sir," said Lewis, gazing down at the set with a certain amount of awe. "My, that's remarkable. It might have been growing there forever."

"It has," said Reinhardt. "I know every tree, every blade of grass in this wood. I have been here half my life. I have lost cities and castles and my home…but this I cannot lose, because this alone is real."

"It…" Lewis blinked, transposing the image of the stage as he had last seen it with its present appearance. "It looks as though it got bigger overnight."

"It needed more trees," said Reinhardt. "I had some dug up and moved."

"Ah," said Lewis. "Dug up. From…?"

Reinhardt made an expansive gesture that took in the surrounding valley. He strolled down the steps toward the stage, where the assistant director was engaged in heated conversation with the actor playing Bottom, as the other actors wandered to and fro along the apron. Lewis ran along behind Reinhardt, feeling curiously uneasy.

Reinhardt seated himself in the front row and, feeling for his reading glasses with one hand, put out the other for the playbook. Lewis handed it to him.

"Look, I have to do this big," argued the actor. "I'm the only one moving on the goddam stage at this point, aren't I?"

Weissberger, the assistant, threw up his hands in impatience. "Not *that* big! You look like you are having an epileptic seizure, Mr. Connolly."

"Baloney!" Connolly clenched his fists. "Look at the size of this house! I'm going to be lucky if anybody at the top even sees *me*, let alone how I play this scene."

"Hmm?" Reinhardt looked over his glasses. "What is their trouble?" he inquired of Lewis, never taking his eyes from the stage. Lewis explained, quickly. Reinhardt got up, leaving the playbook and glasses on the bench, and threaded his way between the lights to the stage. Lewis followed him at two paces' distance.

"Let's see the scene again. Where is the child?" said Reinhardt. Lewis translated, and Mickey Rooney stood up.

"Do we do it again?"

"Yes, please," said Lewis.

"O.K." Rooney walked upstage and hit his mark. With a snort of impatience, Connolly lay down under a tree and sprawled at length.

"And exit Oberon and Titania and..." said Weissberger. Rooney scrambled from behind the tree on hands and knees, and mimed pulling off Bottom's ass's head.

"'*Now-when-thou-wak'st-with-thine-own-fool's-eyes-peep,*'" he recited, and dove back behind the tree.

"Now," said Reinhardt softly, "You must realize that it will be night, you will be well lit, and the whole stage will be yours. They will all be looking at you. You are the last unresolved question." Lewis translated.

Connolly raised his arm, with a galvanic jerk, and waved away imaginary flies. He opened one eye, wide; he opened the other.

"Yes," said Reinhardt, with Lewis echoing him in English, "Yes, all right, you must reach the top of the house, but what then? Go on—"

Connolly sat bolt upright, and stared around wildly. "'*Heigh ho!*'" he shouted. "'*Peter Quince? Flute the bellow-mender?*'" He jumped to his feet, and ran to and fro. "'*Snout the tinker? Starveling? God's my life! Stolen hence, and left me asleep!*'"

"You see? That's—" said Weissberger.

"That's what you call *audible*," said Connolly. Lewis began to translate for Reinhardt, but he put out a hand for silence.

"You see, you are still asleep here," he said. "You are in a dream within a dream. You have only wakened out of the first layer. It is a good dream; you do not yet remember the nightmare. So, no need to jump; you only lean up on your elbow, like a man in his bed, until you come through the next shroud of the dream on *I have had a most rare vision*. Again, please, from the eyes opening."

Lewis translated. Connolly lay down again, opened his eyes, played the scene as requested.

"And *now* you wake a little more and get to your feet," coaxed Reinhardt, "And go on—"

"*'I have had a most rare vision,'*" said Connolly excitedly, jumping upright. He smacked his left fist into his right palm. "*'I have had a dream, past the wit of man to say what dream it was.'*" He stuck an index finger in the air. "*'Man is but an ass if he go about to expound this dream!'*"

"But you are not so awake even now," said Reinhardt. "There is still another layer to come through. You must say this slowly. Sleepily." Lewis translated, and Connolly rolled his eyes.

"Look, *Man is but an ass* is where I get the laugh," he protested. "It's funnier this way." Without waiting for Lewis to translate for him, Reinhardt stepped forward and assumed Bottom's stance. He mimed stretching, murmured the lines in German, and at *past the wit of man to say what dream it was* he yawned elaborately, holding his hand far out as though before an ass's muzzle.

"O.K.," said Connolly, watching him closely. "O.K., that would get a laugh."

"You have been under an enchantment, you have drowned in moonlight, you have been sleeping in the arms of a mist-goddess," said Reinhardt. "And the spell is still on you and you remember now the pleasure, but then the horror sets in too, yes?"

"What'd he say?" Connolly looked at Lewis, who translated.

"Oh." Connolly turned to look at Reinhardt. "So…I get some drama?"

In answer, Reinhardt played the scene through in German. *Methought I was*—and the bewilderment came into his eyes, *there is no man can tell what.* Now he was frightened, feeling his face, feeling the air above his head in case he had ass-ears. *Methought I was, and methought I had*—Reinhardt delivered the lines giggling, weak with relief, and the giggle built to hysterical laughter that culminated in an ass's bray. He froze, as though appalled.

Hesitantly he went on with *But man is but a patched fool if he will offer to say*…and felt again at his face, and scratched his head—was that a tuft of hair, or an ass's ear?…*what methought I had.*

"Yeah!" said Connolly, clapping his hands.

Now Reinhardt mimed silent terror, doubt, confusion, dawning horror. His knees trembled. His frantic hands gripped two long hanks of hair, pulled them upright. Then he released them, stood straight, and swept back his hair. "So. You cannot awake from the nightmare. The audience will feel an echoing scream in their hearts. The wood is the source of all strange beauty, and all fear. The scene is not funny until you wake all the way and know it was only a dream, and then is the catharsis, and *then* you will caper like a fool and make them laugh."

All the actors were watching Reinhardt as though spellbound. Lewis realized his heart was pounding. He swallowed hard and translated, as Reinhardt calmly put his hands in his pockets. Connolly looked from Lewis to Reinhardt, and clapped Lewis on the shoulder.

"Now, that's more like it! Boy, is that a scene." He looked around, triumphantly, at the assistant director. "No wonder they made *him* a professor!"

But as Reinhardt turned away and climbed back to his seat, his face was bleak. "I wanted Charlie Chaplin in that part," he murmured to Lewis. "Why couldn't I have had Charlie Chaplin?"

Three

The nine-mens'-morris is fill'd up with mud

W hen Lewis tucked his copywork under one arm and walked out to his car to drive home, he saw Joseph already in the passenger seat.

"Yes, of course I'll give you a ride home," said Lewis. "How silly of you to make such a fuss about asking, Joseph." He drew nearer, stopped and stared. "Are you all right?"

"No," said Joseph. "I'm screwed. And, much as I'd like to go on a bender at C.C. Brown's with about five hot fudge sundaes, that ain't going to happen. *'I must go seek some dewdrops here, and hang a pearl in every cowslip's ear.'* Can I borrow your car tonight?"

"Why?" Lewis looked anxiously at the Plymouth. "I just had it waxed—"

"I have to break into somebody's house."

"I see." Lewis got into the car. "Phew! I strongly suggest—"

"Yeah, yeah, I know, have a bath first or they'll track me by scent. I was sweating a little more than usual today, OK?"

Lewis started the car and pulled out onto Highland. "Perhaps you ought to tell me what happened."

"It wasn't my fault," said Joseph morosely. "I worked hard on this job, you know? Had this great character I'd made up. 'Joe Wilson.' I had this whole history I'd invented for him. I had pictures of his wife and kids in my wallet. The mortals bought it hook, line and sinker. I made friends with the other guys on the crew. I traded them sandwiches from my dinner pail. We even talked baseball. Like: is Dizzy Dean as good a pitcher as everybody thinks he is? That kind of thing." He grabbed for his hat as they accelerated. "Can we roll up the windows?"

"No. Go on," said Lewis, who had no idea whom Dizzy Dean might be and no inclination to access records on twentieth century baseball just at that moment in any case. Joseph sighed.

"And I might have painted myself green and worn a goddam ballet tutu, for all the good it did me. Did you ever hear of the Tavernier Violet?"

Lewis accessed rapidly. "A diamond? Yes. You're referring to the French Blue? Re-cut as the Hope Diamond."

"Ha! No, I'm not referring to the French Blue. How much of that story do you *really* know?"

Lewis focused in more detail. "Hmmm. 1668, India, one Jean-Baptiste Tavernier bought a crudely-cut 110-carat stone described in color as '*a beautiful violet.*' Sold the stone to Louis XIV, along with several others. Stone recut in 1673, reduced to 69 carats—thereafter called the French Blue. Stolen from the Royal Treasury sometime in mid-September 1792, during the Revolution. Resurfaced twenty years and two days later (just as the Statute of Limitations time ran out) in London, in the possession of Daniel Eliason, recut to 44 carats. Mmmm…George IV acquired it somehow…turned up in the possession of Lord Hope, 1839…sold…sold…

Turkish Sultan…Cartier sold it to Mrs. Evelyn Walsh of Washington, D.C. Well?"

"Anything strike you as funny in that little data stream?"

"Some mortal had remarkable self-control, holding on to it for twenty years," said Lewis, turning left onto Hollywood Boulevard.

"No, Lewis. More basic than that. Access the current description of the stone."

"Weight: 44.5 carats," said Lewis promptly. "Cut: cushion antique brilliant with faceted girdle, extra facets on pavilion. Clarity: VS1. Color: Fancy Dark Steel Blue. Oh. That's not exactly Violet, is it?"

"You bet it isn't," said Joseph.

"So…the Hope diamond, formerly the French Blue, *isn't* the Tavernier Violet," said Lewis. "Well, isn't that fascinating?"

"See—what we have here is another Event Shadow. The blue rock got conflated with the violet one at some point. The blue rock moved on into history and became so famous, with its curse and everything, that it overshadowed the existence of the other stone. Even with the discrepancy in color staring everybody in the face."

"Maybe Tavernier was color-blind," said Lewis.

"He wasn't," said Joseph. "There was an error in the records. 110 carats cut down to 69, doesn't that seem a little drastic to you? And no trace of the remaining 41 carats' worth of violet diamond? Which there wasn't. No, it was recut, all right, but only down to 91 carats. Set in a necklace. Given by the Sun King to his favorite popsy of the moment, Madame de Montespan. And then he asked for it back. He tended to do that kind of thing."

"But she didn't give it back?"

"She didn't. Oh, she brought His Solarness the case, with a big purple fake in it; one that wouldn't have fooled anybody.

Madame, says Louis, *this stone is paste!* She goes white and looks
like she's about to faint. Athenais was a helluva good actress,"
Joseph added, taken for a moment by fond memories. He
shook his head. "She yells, *I have been robbed! It must have been
that dreadful man who repaired the broken clasp for me!* And there
was a lot of smoke and mirrors about some mysterious guy
who'd made off with the real stone. Never happened, though.

"Louis didn't believe her for a minute, but he wasn't
going to push the matter, and she knew she was on the outs
with him by that time anyway, so she didn't care. She kept
the Tavernier Violet. She passed it on to one of her kids by
Louis, so you could say it stayed in the family, the Orleans
branch of it anyhow. Until 1866, by which time it'd found its
way to Mexico."

"And you know all this because...?"

"Because I knew Athenais. And the family passed on the
secret with the stone. And there's a Duke of Orleans who
owns shares in Dr. Zeus."

"You mean they'll hang on into the twenty-fourth century?" Lewis was genuinely impressed. "My, that's tenacity."

"There's a Hapsburg who owns stock, too," said Joseph.

"No!" Lewis sat back. Then he made a face. "Oh, ugh,
you don't suppose they've still got those awful—"

"Yeah, I'm afraid they do."

Lewis shuddered. "I don't want to think about how you
know. But, go on."

"Well, remember where the Lost Treasure comes from in
the first place? One of the jewels donated to the revolution-
ary cause, see, is the Tavernier Violet, which by this time is
in a gold filigree setting.

"What I didn't mention before was the fact that when I
got orders to dig the treasure up and move it, I was supposed
to look for the Tavernier Violet and make sure it was near

the top of the pile, because the Company's going to want it specially retrieved at some point in the near future. I found it; thing looked like a chunk of grape Popsicle.

"Well, I figured I'd make my job a little easier, right? So I stuck the rock in a Mason jar and buried it by itself, right under this one oak sapling, nice and deep."

"Oh, dear," said Lewis. "I have a feeling I know what's coming next." He turned right at Ivar and headed down past the library.

"So, you want to know what happened this morning, after you dropped me off?" said Joseph. "I go running up the canyon with my tail on fire, because I *know* something's gone wrong. You get to be a few thousand years old, you've been around the block a few times, you start to get an instinct for this kind of thing, you know what I'm saying? And here's Cookie's truck zooming down the road toward me, doing maybe forty miles an hour, and I'm thinking—"

"Cookie?"

"Cookie Bernstein. Used to be a cook in the Merchant Marine. He's really got his foot on the gas, and as the truck shoots past me I see Junior kind of slumped over in the bed of the truck—"

"Junior?"

"Junior Macready. Nice kid. Youngest guy on the crew. And he's covered with blood, see? And sort of clutching a hankie right *here*." Joseph slapped himself just above the bridge of his nose. "'Holy Mackerel,' I say to myself, 'that poor kid.' Little do I know! So I get up there finally, panting like a steam engine, and there's Lester and Stinky and Mulligan standing around—"

"What colorful mortal friends you've made—"

"And I forget all about Junior because there's this goddam crane, see, and what's dangling from it, fifteen feet up in the air? Guess. Just take a wild guess," said Joseph, pounding on the dashboard as his fury mounted. "Left! Left turn, Lewis! Jesus Christ on a Ry-Krisp, how could you miss it *again?*"

"You can always catch the streetcar to your burglary, you know," said Lewis. "I'm taking my wild guess now. Was it a certain oak sapling?"

"Except it wasn't a sapling any more," said Joseph. "It had grown into a great big artistically-perfect tree, which *your boss* decided was just the thing for fairies to prance around under. So, this morning, right about when you were driving around this block for the umpteenth time, Max Reinhardt orders my buddies to dig up the oak tree and move it. Here! Park here. This is Mr. Goldfisch's spot, but he's visiting his aunt in Cucamonga."

"But what was all that business about Junior Macready being covered with blood?" said Lewis, as Joseph scrambled out of the car.

"I'm coming to that. Come on; if I don't get out of this lousy undershirt it's going to spontaneously combust," said Joseph, digging in his pockets for his key. Lewis exited the car reluctantly and followed him into the courtyard. It might have been any one of a thousand such places in Los Angeles: an oval of lawn with a single lamp pillar in the center, and, opening off the tiny common area, eight identical cottages, each with a hibiscus bush on either side of its front door.

"Excuse the mess," said Joseph, heading straight for the bathroom. Lewis perched on the edge of a chair in Joseph's tiny furnished parlor and looked around, as Joseph turned on the taps. There wasn't much of a mess actually; there wasn't room.

"How do you live in here?" said Lewis. Joseph shouted from the bathroom:

"Easy. I sleep in the bed and I shave in the bathroom. Mostly I eat in diners and coffee joints."

"But...it's so featureless. Don't you even have books, or pictures of your own?"

"I have a couple of books," said Joseph. "Sentimental value, mostly. Look, Lewis, you know what happens the minute you start accumulating stuff."

There was a splash as he got into the tub and scrubbed vigorously. He went on:

"You get too used to a comfy chair, or a nice view, and you start thinking like a mortal. You get scared to let go of things. You put down roots someplace and, if you're lucky, the Company yanks you out and transfers you halfway around the world. If you're *not* lucky, you stay on for fifty or sixty years and watch all your mortal neighbors die, while the neighborhood goes to hell. Travel light, Lewis, and keep your mind on the job."

"And carry only memories?" said Lewis.

"Not if you can help it," Joseph replied. "They weigh more than ten years' worth of *National Geographic Magazine,* sometimes.

"Anyway, where was I?

"So I go running up to the guys, who are standing around watching the tree like it was a public hanging, and I ask what's going on. Lester says *where you been, you missed all the excitement,* I say *Some jackass wrecked my Ford,* he says *Gee, that's too bad,* and I'm ready to grab him by the throat and choke him but Tex butts in and tells me how they dug down in a circle around this tree with picks and shovels, and then Stinky hooked the crane hoist around the trunk and they all stood back, and first it didn't want to come but then Stinky gave it a real good wrench and *pop,* it just jumped right out of the ground, ten feet straight up.

"Which was when this Mason jar came flying out of the roots and beaned Junior. Busted open and knocked him out cold. And the damn mortal points out the pieces of the Mason jar. I look, but there's no sign of the Tavernier Violet."

"Oh dear," said Lewis, as Joseph rose dripping from the tub and grabbed a towel.

"So there's this know-it-all mortal on the crew, we call him Doc, and he says how the jar must have been shoved down a gopher hole or something by a packrat, because they steal shiny things, like for example the big piece of costume jewelry that came flying out with the jar. *No kidding,* I say, wanting to sit down right there and bawl. And Doc says *oh yes, obviously the piece went missing from some Bowl performance or other back in the '20s.* He had it all doped out, see. *Can I have a look at it?* I query.

"*Oh,* says Mulligan, *we gave it to Junior when he came around. Told him as how since he'd got crowned, he needed some crown jewels.* It had gone right past me in the back of Cookie's truck. The gods look down and laugh." Joseph came out of the bathroom with a towel around his waist, and rummaged in a dresser drawer for underclothes. Lewis averted his eyes.

"How unfortunate. What did you do?"

"Planted the tree where Reinhardt wanted it," said Joseph. "What else could I do? Sweated blood until I saw Cookie coming back in his truck. No Junior with him; naturally we all crowded around and asked questions. The kid's fine, except for twenty stitches in his scalp and a concussion. Cookie dropped him off at his parent's house. He won't be back to work on this job. I found out where he lived so I could send a fruit basket."

"Thoughtful of you," said Lewis.

"I'm not sending the guy a fruit basket, I'm breaking into

his house!" Joseph, decently clad in a pair of drawers, went to his closet and pulled it open.

"How many trenchcoats and fedoras do you own?" said Lewis, staring into the closet.

"Look, I'm a studio dick. A good operative dresses the part, right?" Joseph reached in and pulled out a black turtle-neck sweater. "Here we go. Black shirt, black pants, black sneakers! If I have to burgle somebody's house, I'm going to do it right."

"I'm surprised you don't have a black mask," said Lewis.

"Good point," said Joseph, struck by the idea. "Should I maybe try to get one from Bert Wheeler's?"

"I don't think you can get there before they close," said Lewis. "Anyway, that was sarcasm."

"Cripes, I'm starving. You want to stop at a diner and get a couple of sandwiches before I drop you off?"

"I'll drop you off at your burglary, Joseph, but I'm not loaning you my car," said Lewis. "My case officer's very strict about how many automobiles I'm issued in any one fiscal period."

"Yeah, O.K., I know how that is. You can stick around and be my getaway driver, then."

"Joseph, I've got work to do." Lewis held up the folder of papers he had been clutching. "These have to be copied! They'll be destroyed in an archive fire in 2236, unless I have a good fake to substitute for them."

"2236?" Joseph bent down to tie one sneaker. "Heck, you've got plenty of time, then."

Four

To trust the opportunity of night...

In the end they got hamburger sandwiches wrapped in waxed paper at a stand on the Boulevard, and ate them on a side street below Franklin, a few blocks from Junior Macready's house.

"That's the stuff," said Joseph in satisfaction, tilting his pop bottle for a last swallow. He dropped it on the floor, wadded his sandwich wrapper into a ball and dropped that on the floor too, and sat straight. "O.K! 6700 Yucca. Let's drive by and case the joint."

The area just north of Hollywood Boulevard dated from the time the town had been a teetotaler's colony; it was green-lawn residential, with Eastlake and Craftsman homes set back from a street lined with jacarandas, and every back yard had an orange tree. Plenty of decorative gingerbread and trellises. Men were coming home to dinners; children were playing on the sidewalks, throwing long shadows in the slanting light.

"You're not going to try this until well after dark, I hope," said Lewis fretfully.

"Of course not. 6700! There it is. Make a left up here and park."

Lewis obeyed. They sat staring at 6700 Yucca Avenue. There was a long, long silence.

"I perceive problems," said Lewis at last.

"No kidding," said Joseph, disgruntled.

The house sat on the corner of Yucca and Whitley. It was a big, rambling Craftsman, covered in shingles painted a cheerful yellow. Other than a sprawl of climbing Herbert Hoover roses over the front porch, there wasn't a scrap of concealing vegetation anywhere on the house. Even the requisite citrus tree in the backyard was nowhere near an outer wall.

"Not one iota of lurking space, and all the windows and doors exposed to public view," said Lewis. "And…let's see…I'm picking up ten life forms from inside. Two of which seem to be dogs."

The front door opened. A mortal man emerged, middle-aged but powerfully built, and sat down in a rocking chair on the front porch. He opened out a newspaper and put his slippered feet up on the porch rail. After a moment a mastiff, carrying an immense beef bone, shouldered open the screen door and lay down beside the rocking chair. The dog set to work gnawing on the bone. The bone split with a *crack* that rang out distinctly in the evening air. Joseph shifted in his seat.

"That dog's got good teeth, huh?"

There was a frenzied barking from inside, and a cocker spaniel bounced itself against the screen door three times before bounding out at last, whereupon it raced madly from one end of the porch to the other. The mortal and the bigger dog ignored it. At last a little girl came out and grabbed the spaniel, dragging it back inside.

"A big strong dog and a little yappy dog," said Joseph, rubbing his chin. "And kids. Jeez."

"Is there any chance you got the address wrong?"

Joseph pointed silently to the mailbox, upon which was painted *MACREADY*. Lewis sighed.

Joseph crossed his arms and slouched back in his seat. Lewis leaned his elbows on the steering wheel and set his chin in his palms. Both men closed their eyes, listening, focusing in on the yellow house.

Cracking of bone. Rustling of newspaper pages being turned. Water running; the clatter of dishes being washed. Two mortal voices—young, female—raised over the sound of the water: *So then I told her she could keep her old roller skates. Gosh, did she get mad? I'll say she did, but…*

A click, a squeal, dance music coming over a radio—*the Paul Whiteman Orchestra, ladies and gentlemen!* Feet thundering across a hardwood floor, shrill voices in anger: *Gimme! Give'm back, you dirty bum! Ma! He took my Mickey Mouse!* A female voice cutting in: *Can't I get a moment's peace in this house? Mother, can't you make them understand that I am* talking *on the* telephone?

An older voice, female: *Now, boys, do you want me to take this up with your father?* Another radio switched on, with a higher, tinnier tone: four gunshots and a groan. *Stop shooting, boys; we've caught our jailbird. Thought you'd get away with it, didn't you, mug? Don't you know…*

Creaking, as stairs were climbed. *Junior, dear? Sit up, now; I've brought you a nice glass of grape juice. Oh, you barely touched that soup! Sorry, Ma; I kept spilling it. Thanks. Now, you boys stay out of Junior's room! Gee, you look like you been in the war! Beat it, pipsqueak. Say, what's this thing? Where'd you get a purple diamond?*

It ain't a diamond. It's a piece of fancy glass the guys stuck in my pocket. Some consolation prize, huh?

Can I have it? It'd make a swell hat for Saint Cornelius!

Both Lewis and Joseph opened their eyes and turned to each other, frowning in perplexity.

Sure. Just stop making so much darned noise. Okey-dokey! Oh, dear, this shirt was practically new, wasn't it? Maybe if I soak it with some White King...

"Saint Cornelius?"

Lewis accessed rapidly. "Cornelius the Centurion, pagan convert, first century. Also Pope Cornelius, third century martyr."

"I know! What'd he mean, 'a hat for Saint Cornelius?'"

Lewis shrugged.

"As if this wasn't hard enough," muttered Joseph. "Now I'll have to break into a kid's room. Toys all over the place. Marbles. Jacks. Oh, this is going to be some picnic."

"If you can get inside at all," said Lewis, eyeing the mastiff on the porch.

The man on the porch read his paper until twilight, when he slapped at a mosquito, then rose abruptly and carried his paper indoors. The mastiff followed him. Soft evening fell, lilac-colored and unobtrusive.

There, a light went on in the front parlor; through the window the man could just be glimpsed, in an armchair beside the radio that played dance music. A light in the kitchen window, where the dishes were dried and put away; lights blooming yellow in the upper windows, where someone small was bathed, protesting loudly, and someone else was coached over his schoolwork, and a heated conversation was carried on concerning how stuck-up Mary Ellen Donaldson had become since her aunt had taken her on that trip to France. Someone else was reading a novel, by a pink-shaded lamp; someone else was listening to Cab Calloway in the dark, though the radio cast a dim golden halo on the wall behind it.

Lewis sighed.

"I envy the mortals, sometimes."

Joseph shrugged. He knew the feeling.

"If only they lasted," he said.

"Would their lives be so sweet, if they did?"

"They don't see what we see," said Joseph. "And, hell, we blink, and they're gone. This is what I was talking about! Seven more years, and Junior'll be sweating on an aircraft carrier in the Pacific. The kids'll grow up and go away. There'll be a condo block on this spot in fifty years, the gardens all gone, and you and I will be the only ones who remember these people."

"But we will," said Lewis.

"You think that's a good thing?" said Joseph. "We can't afford to, you know."

It grew late. One by one the upper lights went out; the man in the parlor got up, shut off the radio, and went through the house locking the doors and closing the windows. The immortals heard him climbing a flight of stairs, breathing hard. A light went on, briefly, as teeth were brushed; a light went out. Darkness.

They waited another hour, listening hard for the slowed heartbeats, the quiet breathing or snores that signified everyone slept. When it had been twenty minutes since the last car had passed on the street, Joseph yawned and stretched.

"I guess there's no point in putting it off," he said. "What do you figure? Roof approach? Chimney, maybe?"

"When did you get magic weight-loss powers?" said Lewis. Joseph gave him an aggrieved look.

"Listen, I can flatten myself out like a cockroach when I have to," he said, and got out of the car. "I don't suppose you could give me a hand with the streetlights?"

"I can try," said Lewis. "Best of luck, old man."

Joseph snorted and padded off into the night. Lewis looked at the two nearest streetlights, one halfway down the block and the other on the opposite corner. He bent his head and fixed his attention on the nearer one. He had never attempted this trick, and had no idea if he could really transmit in such a way as to interrupt the circuit.

*Come on, Lewis...*He scowled at the light, massaging the bridge of his nose, rubbing his temples, deep breathing, anything he could think of to focus. There! The light was flickering. Dimming. Yes! Down. Down, but not out...still, he could now make out the pale blue light of the waxing moon.

A faint thump sounded from the direction of the house. Was that Joseph, launching himself at the roof in hyperfunction? Lewis glanced over and saw Joseph poised on the chimney, looking down uncertainly. Joseph looked up, aghast, and Lewis realized that the streetlight had brightened again with his lapse of attention. He turned back immediately and dimmed it once more.

He kept his gaze riveted on the light, forcing himself to concentrate, emptying his mind of all other thoughts...except...Joseph would be covered in soot if he went down the chimney, wouldn't he? Greasy sandwich wrappers and sticky pop bottles were bad enough, but...of course, a mission was a mission, and nothing mattered but the work, and...all the same, maybe it would be best to spread some newspaper out over the upholstery...did he have any newspaper in the trunk? He didn't think he did...oh, wait, he had a road map some over-helpful service station attendant had pressed on him, the last time he'd gotten petrol...no, he was playing an American, mustn't call it that...

There was a crash from the house and a thunder of barking, and a split second later Joseph materialized by the car. He nearly yanked the door off in his haste to scramble in.

"Drive!"

"Wait!" Lewis tore open the glove box and felt around for the map.

"What are you *doing*?"

"You'll get soot all over everything—"

"I didn't go down the chimney!" Joseph threw himself in and pulled the door shut.

"Ow! Get off my arm—"

"Will you drive, for Christ's sake?"

"Did you get it?"

"No—" The barking was still going on, and lights had begun to go on in the house. Lewis started the car and they took off down Whitley, making a right at the Boulevard.

"Shall I circle back and drop you off at your place?" said Lewis hopefully.

"No! Drive around for a while," said Joseph, sounding furious. "We're going to have to go back."

"What happened?"

"Lousy chimney was blocked," said Joseph. "What's the matter with people? Why don't they hire a chimney sweep once in a while? Boy, are they going to get a surprise next time they try to light a fire in there. There must have been three dead crows blocking the flue."

"But you obviously got inside."

"Yeah, somebody left a bedroom window open. So I crawled down the side of the house and hung there a minute, checking it out. The smells were a dead giveaway: bubble gum, cedar pencils and goaty little kid sweat. *Bingo*, I said to myself, and kind of seeped down closer and scanned their breathing and brain rhythms. Two mortal children, males, both of 'em sound asleep. No dogs in the room.

"So I crawled in over the sill and looked around. Right there, on top of this desk, is this shrine made out of a shoebox, with a plaster figure of a saint in it. And guess what's stuck in a lump of plasticine on top of the statue's head."

"The Tavernier Violet," said Lewis. "Oh! It must be *Pope Cornelius*. The papal tiara, don't you see?"

"Who cares which stinking Cornelius it's supposed to be?" Joseph shouted. "It's sitting right next to one of those goddam clockwork monkeys with cymbals, O.K.? And just as I put out my hand, and I swear I didn't even touch the thing, just as I reach for the statue, Bobo the Chimp starts whaling away with the cymbals. Both kids sit up in bed, scream like a couple of bats, and a hundred and sixty pounds of mastiff comes charging down the hall. Exit Joseph, and how!"

"How unfortunate," said Lewis. "What will you do?"

"I'll tell you what we'll do," said Joseph, attempting to calm himself. "We're going to go back there and get inside in broad daylight."

"We aren't," said Lewis firmly.

"No, this will work! Here's what we do. We stake out the place, see, and watch in the morning as everybody leaves, until there's nobody home but the lady of the house and Junior."

"And the two dogs."

"O.K., yes, the two dogs. And then you go up to the front door and ring the doorbell. Meanwhile, I'll be going around the back of the house. The mortal lady opens the door, you ask her if she'd be interested in buying a magazine subscription."

"I'll have to be shouting over the baying of the hounds," said Lewis. "Dogs never like me, you know. They can tell I'm a cyborg, somehow."

"That's the idea! They'll be crazy to get through the screen door so they can kill you, right? And the lady will be apologizing and trying to pull them back—"

"Trying?"

"And if Junior's awake it'll distract him, too, so nobody'll notice me going up the trellis under the kids' room, going in through the window, nabbing the rock and getting out of there, especially if I do it in hyperfunction!" said Joseph. "Problem solved. You tip your hat, thank the lady and exit, meeting me back at the car."

"Pausing only to pry a cocker spaniel off my leg."

"Jeepers, Lewis, be a sport about this, can't you? You're a *cyborg*. You can outrun the dogs."

Five

❖ ❖ ❖

O, I am out of breath in this fond chase...

After a brief stop at the Orchid Apartments, wherein Lewis showered, shaved and put on a clean suit (thoughtfully tucking a can of red pepper into his pocket), they drove back to Yucca Avenue and parked halfway down the block, near enough to watch the front door. Lewis walked down to the Boulevard and returned with a copy of the Citizen-News, and, on climbing behind the wheel once more, opened the paper out, hoping to look as inconspicuous as possible.

At five-thirty the front door opened and the mortal man emerged, carrying a lunch pail.

"That's Macready Senior," said Joseph. "Works as a grip at Paramount. Off to catch the streetcar. One down."

At seven the door opened again and a young lady in a navy blue uniform emerged, carrying an armful of books.

"That's two," said Joseph. "Junior's sister, off to Immaculate Heart High."

At seven-fifteen the door opened again and a swarm of

children emerged, the two girls in navy blue, the two little boys in salt-and-pepper corduroy trousers and white shirts.

"Three, four, five and six," said Joseph in satisfaction. "That's it. Off to school, kiddies."

But instead of parading off in the direction of the street-car tracks, the children lined up expectantly by the mailbox.

"Perhaps they take the schoolbus?" said Lewis, folding up his paper.

"Crap!" Joseph sat bolt upright, staring at the older of the two boys. Lewis looked, then looked more closely.

"Oh," he murmured. The mortal child was clutching an open shoebox, converted to a shrine by means of stained glass windows drawn in crayon, housing a small plaster statue.

"He's taking the damn thing to school!"

"Is that it?" Lewis intensified his focus. He made out the winking point of violet on the statue's head, just before a yellow schoolbus pulled up to the curb and blocked his view. "Yes, that's Pope Cornelius, all right, although he's had to make over a statue of St. Jude; I don't suppose there are a lot of St. Cornelius statues around. But his feast day is September 16, which is this Sunday, so—"

"Lewis, would you mind very much starting the car and following that bus?" said Joseph, slowly and carefully.

"There's no need for sarcasm," said Lewis, starting the car.

The schoolbus trundled along for some blocks, stopping often, difficult to shadow discreetly; but at last it pulled into a vast schoolyard just above Sunset. Lewis and Joseph pulled up and watched as the stream of children emerged from the bus and assembled in ranks before marching into the school.

"Cripes, the place looks like a fortress," said Joseph. "Circle around. Let's see if there are any windows."

Lewis obliged. He found a spot a block away to the east that provided them with a clear view of the eastern wall of the school: six windows, three on the first story and three on the second. In each was framed an identical classroom: four straight rows of desks occupied by thirty-six uniformed children. Only the ages of the inmates differed, room by room, with a certain slump noticeable in the shoulders of the oldest ones. Joseph and Lewis regarded them in silence.

"Then again, sometimes I don't envy mortals at all," said Lewis. "Slotted in like so many little machine parts. How can they bear it?"

Joseph shrugged. He pointed to the middle classroom on the first floor. There, on a table, was a veritable choir of plaster saints. Some were glued into abalone shells, some were mounted on pedestals made of painted tomato cans; there at the back was St. Cornelius, with his violet crown.

"O.K., this isn't so bad," said Joseph. "We can come back here tonight and break into the place."

"You're going to desecrate a shrine?" said Lewis.

"What do you care? You were a Roman, not a Roman Catholic. It isn't like Saint Cornelius is going to lean down and pitch a thunderbolt at you."

"No, but the mortals believe in that sort of thing, and that can make a remarkable difference," said Lewis. "Besides, it's rather an endearing idea, don't you think? This whole little pantheon of minor saints, looking out for the welfare of humanity? For example, Pope Cornelius is the one you pray to to keep away earaches. I find that charming."

"You must have slept through the Reformation, huh?"

"No, I missed that century. I was Guest Services Director at New World One back then. Wouldn't it be a nicer world, really, if the mortals had someone to watch over them?"

"Maybe, but all they have is us. Mind taking me back to

my place so I can get changed for work? And, uh, giving me a lift to the Bowl, afterward?"

"Doesn't Mr. Mayer wonder where you've got to?"

"He thinks I'm visiting my mother in Altoona."

Theseus and Hippolyta came hand in hand across the great creaking trestle, leading the splendid if half-costumed wedding procession. Ignoring them, an electrician and his assistant went up and down ladders among the trees, installing the tiny flickering lights that would, on opening night, impersonate fireflies. The assistant stage manager counted out beats, over the faint whine of a Victrola playing Mendelssohn's *Wedding March* beside his chair. It creaked to a close just as the royal couple stepped onstage. He turned and flashed Reinhardt a thumbs-up.

"You see?" said Reinhardt, dabbing the sweat from his brow with a handkerchief. "It is perfectly timed, and nobody fell off."

"I do trust there will be a handrail of some sort, before performance?" said Theseus, with frosty *noblesse oblige*. He was being portrayed by John Lodge, a Boston aristocrat who had briefly condescended to the thespian life.

"But the point of the ramp is that it's just supposed to sort of hang there, like magic," protested the assistant director. Reinhardt looked back and forth between them until Lewis translated.

"A skilled actor is half acrobat," he said in response. "But if he is frightened, have the crew string up hand ropes. Black velvet ones."

Lewis repeated this in English, slightly edited, and the production manager threw up his hands in despair.

"Black velvet ropes? Where am I supposed to get those?"

"Theater supply wholesaler?" Lewis suggested. "Costume department?"

Miss Sibley, Lewis's immediate superior in the ranks of Reinhardt's assistants, fanned herself with a copy of the *Los Angeles Times*. She looked out at the hills beyond the Bowl and said doubtfully: "But in the actual performance, they'll have to come all the way down from up there, won't they? Carrying lit torches? My, that'll be dangerous, with all that dry brush."

"The Fire Department gave him a permit," said Lewis. "And he's going to time it again at Dress Rehearsal."

"Oh," she said, but not as though convinced.

The crowds of attendants filed onto the set, and lined up a little awkwardly on the turf. Weissberger turned to look at Reinhardt, who smiled and nodded. "Please," he said. "Go on."

The action of the play went forward—lovers forgiven, pomp and ceremony, and in came Bottom and his mates to present their play-within-the-play, *Pyramus and Thisbe*. Lewis leaned forward in his seat, in anticipation. He had seen some four hundred and seventy-three performances of *A Midsummer Night's Dream*, over the centuries, and *Pyramus and Thisbe* just got funnier every time he saw it.

The Prologue was spoken, the Wall spoke his piece. Enter Pyramus and Thisbe (Walter Connolly in rattling armor, Sterling Holloway in demure drag). The lovers swore to be true through the Wall's chink, and the fatal assignation at Ninny's Tomb was arranged. Exit Lovers and Wall; enter Lion and Moonshine, Moonshine being personified by Otis Harlan, best known later as the voice of Happy the Dwarf in *Snow White*. Enter Thisbe once more, Lion roars; Thisbe screams and flees, dropping Veil, which is promptly seized and rent by Lion. Exit Lion; enter Pyramus, leaping to conclusions and a death scene of epic awfulness. Shakespeare, perverting all his genius to write as badly as possible!

Reinhardt shifted in his seat. He stood and advanced a few steps down toward the stage. The suppressed giggles of the other actors fell silent at once.

"This is good," he said, "but I think it would be funnier if Thisbe is more bulky, more the big plowboy. Can you try it that way?" Lewis opened his mouth to translate, but the actor playing Quince (Frank Reicher) relayed the request first.

"But he isn't a plowboy, Professor Reinhardt," said Holloway. "Francis Flute is a bellows-mender." He mimed pumping a pair of bellows. "It says so in the script."

Reicher translated. Reinhardt frowned. He looked away, waving his hand.

"Then I would like to see you play it bigger. More the country bumpkin."

"I'll do my best," said Holloway. He squared his shoulders manfully.

"Please, go on, then," Reinhardt said. Under his breath he murmured, "It would have been so much funnier with W.C. Fields." He turned and climbed back to his seat. The actors watched him with a certain amount of resentment. Harlan sidled up to Holloway and thumped him on the shoulder.

"What the heck," Harlan piped cheerfully. "You can go have yourself some fun tonight and forget the old—"

Miss Sibley leaned toward Lewis, and unpursed her lips long enough to whisper: "This is dreadful. Don't they realize the Professor is one of the giants of German romantic theater? The studios ought to have leaped at the chance to loan him their stars!"

Lewis looked sympathetic, but shrugged. "Plebeians, I suppose. It'll all work out on the night."

Six

Wherefore was I to this keen mockery born?...

The evening star was just visible when the Plymouth pulled up outside the school above Sunset. Joseph scrambled out of the car and closed its door. He had once again dressed in his all-black ensemble.

"Why don't you just circle the block a few times, O.K.?" he said. "Less conspicuous." Lewis sighed, shook his head, and pulled out from the curb.

He was on his fifth circumnavigation when he picked up the frantic transmission:

Lewis! Corner of Selma and Cherokee! Step on it!

Lewis, already headed down Selma, gunned the motor accordingly and a moment later drew level with Joseph, who vaulted into the passenger seat and pointed in the direction of a rapidly-disappearing Model T. "After that guy!" Joseph shouted.

A thrilling car chase did not ensue, because the Model T proceeded up to the Boulevard and joined the slow procession of evening traffic in a westerly direction. Joseph did not, therefore, go into Action Cyborg mode and leap from the front seat of the Plymouth to the roof of the Model T and rip it open like so much paper, hauling his quarry out to deliver a lethal karate chop. Real cyborgs seldom get the chance to do that sort of thing, and never in front of several hundred mortal witnesses.

"What happened this time?" said Lewis, waiting for the STOP signal to swing down out of sight.

"It started out easy," said Joseph, peering ahead at the Model T, now separated from them by a slow-moving touring car. "Go! Go! Come on! Transom window in the second-floor boy's bathroom left open a crack. I got it open, squeezed though headfirst, ran downstairs to the kid's classroom. The shrine was right where it ought to be, all right, but somebody'd pinched the diamond."

"How do you know it was this person?" Lewis inquired, trying to pass the touring car.

"Because I switched to thermal vision, O. K.? And there were all these fading green and orange steps going up and down the aisles, and brighter steps going up to the table with the shrines, and a big red handprint around Saint Pope Cornelius and a thumbprint right in the middle of his face, and flaming red prints going away from the table again and out the classroom door!

"So I ran after them. They went all the way down the hall, and right there at the end was this big door with window panes. On the other side of it was this mortal, all lit up like Satan, locking the door and putting his keys in his pocket."

"Must be the school janitor," said Lewis.

"So I scrammed, and just as I was sticking my head out the bathroom window I saw the guy getting into his car."

"Oh, dear, he's probably headed for a pawnshop," said Lewis.

"Crap. Well, I know what we'll do. You rear-end the guy as hard as you can. I'll jump out—"

"Joseph, this car is Company property!"

"So are you."

"And I'm cheaper to repair!"

"Lewis, for Christ's sake—Right! Make a right! He's going up LaBrea!"

Lewis cranked the wheel and they followed the Model T uphill as far as Franklin, where it pulled to the curb and parked. They cruised past it as a mortal emerged. But for his grubby overalls and undershirt, he might have been a Prussian officer or a headwaiter at some particularly snooty restaurant; he had an upright bearing and meticulously waxed moustaches.

Joseph, glaring at him as they passed, said: "That's the school janitor, all right."

"Oh, my gosh!" said Lewis. "That's not all he is! Don't you recognize him?"

"No."

"Access a record of male film stars for the years 1910 to 1925!"

Joseph obeyed, as Lewis took them up to LaBrea Terrace and turned around. "Larry Montcalm? Jeepers, that was *Larry Montcalm*? He used to make three grand a week over at Selig Polyscope!"

"Lo, how the mighty are fallen," said Lewis. He pulled to the curb and parked, setting the hand brake, as Joseph stared at the mortal.

"I bet he's going to change his clothes and hock the diamond. Where's he going?"

They watched as Montcalm entered the vestibule of a brownstone on the corner. Joseph got out of the car. "You stay here."

"Gladly," said Lewis. Joseph strode down the street, looking determined, and vanished into the brownstone. A moment later he came running back uphill.

"Goddammit, he lives in the basement! Go down and park on Franklin."

Lewis groaned, but obeyed. By the time he had found a parking space, Joseph was ready to leap from the car in his agitation.

"Look at that! Could the basement windows be any more exposed? Right out on the sidewalk, for crying out loud! So much for a surreptitious entrance that way. Can you pick him up at all?"

"Sssh!" Lewis waved a hand distractedly, squeezing his eyes shut as he focused on the basement windows. Clinking, rattling, rustling, the sound of running water, a single mortal heartbeat…"He's alone, at least. Seems to be taking a bath."

"O.K.; I'll have to go in and knock on his door," said Joseph. "Though I don't look like a cop, in this getup… crumbs. *You* could pass for one, though. Look, why don't you go knock on his door and tell him you're a plainclothes cop—"

"What, from the Parochial School Patrol? How would anybody but us know he stole anything, at this point?"

"You could say you're a G-Man, and you've been tailing him on suspicion of being a Socialist or something—"

Lewis had several objections to this plan, and during the time they were bickering over alternate strategies the mortal finished his bath, got dressed and was humming to himself as he made noises suggestive of preparing a light meal.

"O.K.," said Joseph at last, "then you're going to have to drive me to a market where I can buy about ten boxes of Cracker Jack, because—"

"Wait! Was that his doorbell that just rang?"

They both focused on the basement. Yes; they heard footsteps crossing the floor, and then:

"Muriel, dearest! You're a little early; I'm afraid I was just sitting down to dine. Don't you look ravishing in that charming ensemble, though!"

It was a high voice with a peculiar throttled intonation, the sort best suited to cartoon characters. Martians in tennis shoes, perhaps.

"Well, that explains why his career didn't survive the Talkies," said Joseph.

"You look swell, yourself. Do you really like it?" said another mortal voice, female, not young, a little breathless. "I took the hem up a couple of inches, just like you said. And I made the hat myself, out of an old brocade cushion—"

"Delightful. Delightful. Yes, we'll be the sinecure of all eyes!" The male mortal sounded sly. "Particularly since…but where are my manners? May I offer you a plate of Campbell's?"

"Oh, no thanks, dear, I had a sandwich before I came over. I'm too nervous to eat much anyhow. Say, look at the right sleeve, here. Does it look like I got that stain out?"

"Why, it's like new! No one could tell, I assure you. And, under the circumstances, I doubt anyone will be looking at your *arm*, dear Muriel."

"Why, whatever do you mean, Lawrence?"

Joseph, who had been slouched down in the car seat, sat bolt upright. "Oh, no," he said.

"What?" said Lewis.

"All in good time, Muriel, all in good time. If you'll permit me—"

"Oh, sure, you go right ahead and finish your soup."

"I have this bad feeling about how Lawrence is planning to impress dear Muriel," said Joseph. Lewis intensified his focus and listened in. There was gallant small talk interspersed with the sound of soup being consumed, there were modest replies, there were the sounds of china being cleared away, and then:

"Oh! Lawrence, you shouldn't have!"

"Uh-oh," said Lewis.

"Nonsense. I saw this trifle, and I said to myself: 'That's the very thing for my Columbina!'"

"'Columbina'?" said Joseph.

All was made plain when, after fifteen more minutes of coy chatter, the mortals exited the building and came into view on the corner, where they looked both ways before crossing to Lawrence's Model T.

"Oh, *Harlequin* and Columbina," said Lewis. Joseph said something unprintable. Lawrence wore a diamond-patterned suit of blue and green, with a black domino mask; his lady friend wore a frilly skirt and jacket in a matching diamond pattern in purple and lavender. A mortal could not have made it out at that distance, but to cyborg vision it was painfully clear: there around her neck, on a chain, was a flashing violet light, brilliant as a movie starlet's eyes.

"Of all the lousy luck!" Joseph leaned forward and beat his forehead against the dashboard a few times.

"Stop that! You'll dent it. They're driving away, you know. Shouldn't we be following them?"

"Sure. Why not?" said Joseph listlessly.

Lewis started the car again and raced after the Model T. He followed it all the way to Highland and up past the Hollywood Bowl, by which time Joseph had recovered himself enough to be plotting again.

"O.K., all is not lost. The next time they pull up at a traffic signal, I'll leap out and grab the rock through the window. I'll run off into the bushes and up over the hill, you make a u-turn and pick me up again out on Mulholland—"

"What if they get my license number and call the police?"

"Then we'll ditch the car on Mulholland and you can report it as stolen—heads up, there's a traffic signal! Get ready! "

"Joseph, I've only had this car six months, and—"

"Dammit!" Joseph clutched his hair and pulled, in his frustration. Rather than stopping at the signal, the Model T had turned onto a side street that climbed steeply, paralleling Cahuenga. "No! Go after 'em!"

Lewis swerved to follow, neatly and narrowly missing an oncoming truck, whose driver shook his fist and pounded on the horn. The street climbed, and climbed; leveled out briefly and then climbed some more, throwing in a curve for good measure. A spectacular view of the Cahuenga Pass and the San Fernando valley beyond opened out to the right, but there was no time to admire the scenery. As Lewis was shifting gears, Joseph pointed and yelled. "There!"

To their left, a number of cars were parked along the street, and the Model T was performing the profoundly chancy maneuver of turning around in a driveway just under a blind curve. Lewis slowed his car to watch as the Model T completed the turn safely and pulled in behind the other cars, from which other costumed mortals were emerging.

"It must be a studio party," said Lewis. "Look! There's Charlie Chase. And there's one of the Cherry Sisters, and Ralph Falconer...that's Richard Talmadge, he was a stunt-man around the same time I was."

"Huh," said Joseph, looking thoughtfully up at the house to which the mortals were climbing. It sat at least eight flights of zigzagging stairs above the street, and was a sprawling, manyleveled Spanish-style place, with balconies and gardens. "Big house, lots of guests in masks, lots of booze flowing. I could crash it! I just need a costume."

"Where are you going to get a costume at this hour on a Friday night?"

Joseph snapped his fingers. "Last-Minute Lester's!"

"I beg your pardon?"

"A little Industry secret. He's on Curson Street. Let's go!"

As they were headed back downhill through the Cahuenga Pass, Joseph explained: "This guy worked in Wardrobe at most of the little studios. When a shoot wrapped, he used to take one or two of the costumes back to his place and forget to return them, you know what I mean? So he built up a collection. He pays for mothballs by renting out costumes to people in the know."

Fifteen minutes later they pulled up in front of a modest bungalow on a tree-lined street. Lewis waited in the car as Joseph went to the door; it was opened by a gaunt man cradling a small poodle in his arms. Joseph went inside.

Half an hour later Lewis looked into the rear view mirror and beheld Joseph approaching the car. Startled, he turned around and stared out the window.

"God Apollo! What on earth—"

"It was all he had left tonight," said Joseph. "That a guy could wear, anyhow. Just shut up and let me in the car, O.K.?"

He wore a skin-tight black body suit, black pumps with spats, and white gloves. Lewis thought he might be impersonating Mickey Mouse, until noting the cane and bulky papier-mâché body under Joseph's arm.

"Mr. Peanut?"

"Yeah. Can we get this damn thing in the back seat? I'm not riding through the night wearing it."

Lewis got out and rolled down the window, but the giant peanut shell wouldn't go through; nor could he get the passenger seat tilted far enough forward to push it into the back.

"It's not going to fit in the boot, either," he said. "I'm afraid you'll have to put it on. Cheer up! It's not as though anyone will recognize you."

Muttering viciously to himself, Joseph lifted the peanut shell and struggled into it.

"Can you take his little top hat off?" Lewis asked. "Otherwise you'll have to ride sort of bent over."

"No, the damn hat is built in," said Joseph, a bit muffledly. He got his arms out through the appropriate holes at last. "Boy, this is some tight squeeze. At least I can see O.K. Well, fairly O.K. Where's the cane?" He spotted it on the grass and bent to pick it up. There was a sound richly evocative of cyborg flesh bursting through overstrained elasticized cotton-silk fabric. It was followed by a burst of profanity in Neolithic proto-Euskaran.

"Oh, dear," said Lewis.

"Does it show?" Joseph turned to and fro.

"No, you're all right—can you get the shell off again?"

Joseph peered down at himself. "Not without getting arrested."

He climbed awkwardly into the front seat, accompanied by more ominous sounds of fabric tearing. "Just drive, Lewis."

There were at least six traffic signals on the way back to the party, and Joseph shrank farther down into the seat at each stop, though Lewis merely smiled and waved at his fellow motorists when they stared. Not soon enough, they came back to the high winding street above which the house sat.

"My, they're in full swing," said Lewis, gazing up at the house. Every window was lit, and the sound of music and laughter floated forth.

"So much the better, huh?" said Joseph, groping for his cane. "Why don't you just let me off here, and park someplace close and wait? I'm not walking back to Morningside in this getup."

Lewis had to open the door for him, after which Joseph crawled out, straightened up and began his resolute climb of the first of the flights of steps. Lewis found a parking space halfway down the block below, and pulled in to wait.

It was dark, and quiet. The sloping lot on the other side of the street was dense with old trees, which filtered out traffic sounds from the Cahuenga Pass below. A single swaying bulb hung from a telegraph pole, halfway down the block, giving no particular competition to the crescent moon and stars. Lewis yawned. He settled himself into a more comfortable position and folded his arms.

"'Oh, weary night, oh long and tedious night/ Abate thy hours! Shine comforts from the East/ That I may back to Athens...'" he murmured to himself. Now, *that* would be pleasant. He'd liked Athens, when he'd been stationed there in the third century. There'd been a nice little wine-shop just off the School of Philosophy that had been a great place to relax with a scroll. Really quite a lot like California, at least in the quality of the light, that hot bright shimmer...

And of course there hadn't been any Wood near Athens, more's the pity, unless you counted olive groves. Too thickly settled, even in the third century...there might have been a wood a league without the town in Theseus' day, but it wouldn't have resembled Shakespeare's English forest...rocky hills like Hollywood's, instead, with the same live oaks, and whatever the Mediterranean equivalent of sagebrush was...actually rather a lot like what Reinhardt had built, down the pass. Lewis wondered if he realized it?

He yawned again and let his primary consciousness fade to standard maintenance, while his secondary consciousness sorted through the day's work. He found it easy to forge

Reinhardt's handwriting, but much more difficult to reproduce his sketches. Something to do with being a cyborg, perhaps. It was curious that Company operatives, though responsible for salvaging and preserving so much great art, seemed incapable of any creativity themselves...

Lewis was analyzing chromatic value in a watercolor study of the Faery Court when he was roused to primary consciousness by lights flaring behind him. He peered into the rear view mirror. A car was being started; someone leaving the party. Perhaps he ought to pull into the spot they had vacated?

As he was watching the other car's tail lights diminish down the hill and trying to decide whether to move, something hit the rear of the Plymouth with a *thump*. A second later Joseph had yanked the passenger door open and was frantically squeezing his costumed bulk into the seat.

"Go!" he shouted.

"Did you get it?"

"No. Follow that car!"

"But that wasn't Larry Montcalm—"

"I know! It was *another* thief!"

Lewis threw the Plymouth into neutral and coasted forward, starting the engine on the way down the hill. Joseph, gasping inside the papier-mâché peanut head, finally caught his breath enough to say—well, nothing that would edify the sensitive reader. When he had finished venting, however, he added:

"Arnaud Fletcher!"

"What, the gossip columnist?" They reached the bottom of the hill. The other car was nowhere in sight. Lewis, peering about uncertainly, switched to thermal vision and picked up the car's track—heading not down into Hollywood, but up Mulholland Drive. He followed.

"Yeah," said Joseph. "I was so close! No trouble getting in, at least once I'd got up all those damn stairs. I found a bathroom window open on ground level. Flushed the toilet and walked out bold as brass. Nobody even noticed. The gin was flowing free, let me tell you. All kinds of Industry old-timers there. Half the people who used to work at Edendale and box-lunch extras of DeMille's.

"They were pretty lively, for a bunch of has-beens; there was this big front room where they'd pushed all the furniture to the edges and rolled up the rugs, and they were dancing to Victrola records. Which made it hell to get through the room, see, which I had to do because Harlequin and Columbina were doing the Lindy clear across on the other side. So I just sort of insinuated myself out on the dance floor and tapped some guy on the shoulder, and there I was Lindy-hopping with this dame dressed as Marie Antoinette when this dog came leaping in!"

"He cut in on you?" Lewis inquired, steering around a curve with a precipitous drop on one side.

"No, not a guy dressed as a dog; a real dog! A Saint Bernard!"

"Oh, dear. And I guess he wanted to rend you limb from limb?"

"No; this one couldn't tell I was a cyborg. He was a *happy* dog. He loved me. In the least dignified way imaginable, O.K.? Marie Antoinette broke away from me, just shrieking with laughter, which pretty much blew my plan of unobtrusively partner-swapping my way across the dance floor to Columbina's arms.

"There was this sideboard at one edge of the room with canapés and drinks and stuff, so I went over there with the dog still lurching all over me. I grabbed a martini for myself and dropped him a couple of deviled eggs; did he lose interest in me? Not a chance. He jumped up and tried to put his forelegs around my neck. Then he noticed my martini, and dove into it nose-first."

"He spilled your drink?"

"No, he drank it! The mutt was drunk! That was why he was so goddammed happy. You know what drunk dog breath smells like?"

"Please don't tell me." Lewis peered forward, straining to make out the fading heat trail that wound on ahead.

"So I set about three martinis on the floor for him and he ceased waxing amatory, thank the gods, just started lapping 'em up, and I looked around to see Harlequin Larry and Columbina Muriel retiring from the dance floor to a settee in a nice dark corner. I pushed through the crowd and worked my way along the wall, sort of over and around the furniture. I overheard all kinds of snippets of conversation that would make me a fortune, if I was inclined to blackmail somebody.

"In fact—" Joseph pounded his fists on the dashboard. "In fact, I remember Arnaud Fletcher talking about this other party that's going on tonight! That must be where the son-of-a-bitch is headed!"

"Well, where is it?" asked Lewis. A vista of Hollywood opened out to the left, a carpet of lights glittering as far as the sea; but up here was night and silence, and the occasional coyote blinking in the beam of the Plymouth's headlights.

"He didn't say! Except that it's at 'Jack's place,' wherever that is. Supposedly it's one wild party. 'Plenty of hot stuff, brother, and I do mean hot,' he said. He said it just like that, *insinuating*, you know?"

"I suppose he meant cocaine or something," said Lewis, as they came to the intersection of Outpost and Mulholland. Down or up? He focused and made out the tracks continuing up along Mulholland, though they were fading fast as the night air cooled them. He followed as fast as he dared.

"I guess. Or hookers. Anyway I managed to get over near the settee at last. It had been pushed up against a table and a couple of other pieces of furniture, so there was some space behind it, see? And I pretended to pass out and fall over, which nobody even noticed. In fact, there were already a couple of drunks snoring away in various corners back there. I crawled close up under the table until I was right behind Larry Montcalm and Muriel Whoever, and scanned 'em."

"That must have been a little difficult in a peanut costume," said Lewis, slowing the car as he studied the thermal track of his quarry. The other vehicle had left Mulholland and driven up a straight dirt track leading to a still higher elevation. Gingerly he urged the Plymouth forward.

"You're telling me, brother! But I thought I'd gotten lucky at last, because Larry had Muriel's feet in his lap and was rubbing her bunions, and she was lying back right above me in a sort of ecstatic state. I was able to rise up on my hands and sneak a peek; sure enough, neither of them noticed me. And there was the Tavernier Violet, hanging around the dame's neck on a dime-store chain—Say, watch out!"

"I'm sorry," said Lewis, through his teeth rather. "Plymouth doesn't equip their cars with mountain goat feet."

"Jeepers, what kind of idiot would build a house up here?" Joseph looked around. "See, if I hadn't been wearing the peanut suit I could have just hooked my cane through the chain, flipped the damn thing up and grabbed the stone, and been out one of the windows before anybody could yell. I wasn't any too sanguine about running blind down all those steps, though. Muriel was pretty far gone in bliss, so I figured I could try a little stealthy theft instead. I pulled off a glove with my teeth and got my finger and thumb on the catch, and managed to unfasten it.

"But right then somebody put on *The Charleston*, and what did Muriel do but sit up squealing about how that's her favorite dance. She grabbed Larry by the hand and jumped out on the dance floor. I scrambled to my feet and—look out! Jesus, Lewis, you want to end up at the bottom of a cliff?"

"I don't think I can turn around here," said Lewis, gazing out into the black ravine that yawned before the Plymouth's front bumper.

"Come on, then," said Joseph, getting out of the car. Lewis set the hand brake and got out too. "Hey hup ho—"

Between them the two immortals lifted the car and walked in a half-circle. "So I jumped over the back of the couch," Joseph continued, "*Just* in time to see the Tavernier Violet go bouncing off Muriel's chest onto the dance floor. She didn't notice it. I Charlestoned my way out into the madding throng, hoping to do a quick dip and grab it, but Larry (who didn't notice it'd fallen either) kicked it, in a burst of terpsichorean frenzy, and it went skating across the floor, trailing its chain, *ping ping ping* in a series of bank shots off mortal feet, and ended up right under the nose of Mr. Arnaud Fletcher, who was dressed like Valentino in *The Sheik*, by the way."

"Just hold it there a moment, won't you?" Lewis climbed back in the car and shifted gears.

"Sure." Joseph held the car in place with one hand, then gave it a push as Lewis stepped on the gas. The car teetered for a moment and then climbed effortfully toward a still-narrower and more steep trail, with Joseph plodding alongside. "Where was I? So Arnaud Fletcher looked down, saw the rock at his feet. He stooped on it like a duck on a june bug, whammo, and stashed it in his robes. He exited the party, I exited in hot pursuit, slightly delayed because my big friend the Saint Bernard noticed me again and wanted to pitch some woo. By the time I found Fido another drink and got out the door, the damn mortal was at the bottom of the stairs and heading for his car."

"Er—" Lewis trod on the brake and leaned out the window. "I can't get up this goat path, I'm afraid. But I think we've found the other party, Joseph."

"What? Oh." Joseph looked up the trail. The moonlight was glinting off a number of automobiles, parked somewhat precariously on the side of the precipice. Beyond them rose something that looked remarkably like the dome of a mosque.

"Joseph," said Lewis, "are those drumbeats?"

Joseph turned to listen, then shifted irritably inside the peanut suit until his ear was a little closer to the eye-holes.

"Yeah. They're darabukas," he said. "What have they got going up there, a Rudolph Valentino Memorial lodge?"

"It smells like someone's barbequing a goat," said Lewis, wrinkling his nose.

"That's lamb. And cannabis. Great. O.K., I'm not going to try anything subtle this time. I'll march in there, find Fletcher, sock him, roll him and run for it. You'd better keep the engine running."

Lewis looked around. "Should I really wait right *here*? If I try to clear that rut at anything over five miles an hour, I'll break an axle."

"So it isn't the best spot for a quick getaway," Joseph admitted. Hastily he accessed a topographical map of the area, then transmitted a set of coordinates to Lewis. "There you go! See that ridge, right behind the dome thing? The hill drops down on the other side to Pacific View. You wait right below; I'll scram down the hill once I've got the rock, and we'll be away before the mortals can get their cars started."

"Oh, that's a much better idea," said Lewis, noting with relief that Pacific View was at least paved. "Good luck! I'm off."

"See you in the funny papers," said Joseph gloomily. Lewis let out the clutch, threw the Plymouth into neutral and braked his way down the hill until the front wheels were on solid pavement. He coasted down and around to the coordinates Joseph had sent him, and pulled up, carefully turning the front wheels into the curb.

Worriedly he scanned the Plymouth, checking for indications of metal fatigue or excessive automotive wear. Yes; he was going to have to take it in to have the wheels aligned. A lube job wouldn't do it any harm, either. The transmission seemed to be all right, which was miraculous, after that last climb, but perhaps he'd ask the mechanic to have a look at the clutch.

He sat there in the dark for a moment as a gnawing conviction grew that a twig had gotten stuck in the radiator grille on that last overgrown trail. At last he got out and walked around the front of the car. Yes; yes, there was one, wedged in firmly. Shaking his head, Lewis took out his penknife and became absorbed in working the twig out.

It took a great deal of care to avoid scratching the paint or puncturing the radiator, and so he was only dimly paying attention to the drumbeats that sounded on the night air, with the occasional drunken catcall.

He was polishing the headlights with his pocket handkerchief when the drums suddenly stopped. There was an outcry. Lewis craned his head back to look up the hill and saw a giant peanut plummeting toward him.

"Thank all the gods," he said, and ran around the car to get behind the wheel. As he rounded the fender, however, he was momentarily blinded by the lights of a car speeding down Pacific View toward him. He blinked away the after-image as it passed; a convertible, and something oddly familiar about the driver...

Over the roar of the starting engine he heard the patter of feet as Joseph ran frantically toward the car, and felt the lurch as Joseph leaped on the running board.

"Follow that car!" Joseph bawled through the window, pointing after the convertible. "Again."

"But that wasn't Arnaud Fletcher." Lewis cranked the wheels away from the curb and stepped on the gas. Joseph clung to the passenger door.

"No! It's Sterling Holloway!"

"What?" Lewis replayed his glimpse of the passing car. "Sterling Holloway!"

"*Thisbe* Sterling Holloway? What was *he* doing—"

"Lewis, shut up and drive!"

Lewis pursed his lips, and drove as fast as he dared with Joseph, screaming imprecations into the night, on the Plymouth's running board. The convertible sped ahead of them, around the curve and down the long hill that dropped to the floor of the Pass. Finally back on the long straightaway of Cahuenga, they began to close the gap. The taillights of the convertible had just begun to draw appreciably closer when Lewis heard the warning siren coming from behind them.

The traffic cop nearly wet himself laughing, but gave them a speeding ticket anyway.

Seven

❖ ❖ ❖

What, a play toward? I'll be an auditor…

"We're lucky you didn't get us arrested," said Lewis, sullenly kicking at fragments of peanut costume.

"So I was a little sore," said Joseph, shouting from the bathroom. "It'll be O.K. anyhow. All you'll have to do is excuse yourself during the next rehearsal, run out to Holloway's car and search around for the rock. Easy."

"No, it won't be," said Lewis. He opened Joseph's kitchen cabinet and scowled at the contents. "I'm Mr. Reinhardt's translator, remember? *You* go search for the damned thing. Haven't you any Ovaltine?"

"What?"

"Ovaltine!"

"No. Make some cocoa or something."

"No, thank you. I still have to drive home."

"Here." Joseph strode out of the bathroom in his shorts, opened a drawer, dug out a bottle of single malt and poured a pair of shots into a coffee cup and a juice glass respectively.

❖ 79 ❖

"Now it's breakfast. Look, I am a total innocent in this tribulation of cosmic proportions. Are you going to let me tell what happened or what?"

"Go on, then." Lewis had a sip of whiskey, breathed out fumes, and converted the sip to water and complex sugars.

"So there I was, sneaking up the trail toward the faux mosque or whatever it was," said Joseph. He downed his whiskey in a gulp. "I was hearing glasses clinking, mortals laughing, all kinds of stag-party hubbub. I couldn't hear Fletcher at first, until he came in loud and clear saying: *There! What do you think of that?*

"And this dame says in reply, *Oooh, Arnie, it's beautiful! Can I wear it?*

"Whereupon this third mortal chimes in, *Hell yeah! It can be the Eye of the Spider-God or something! We'll rewrite the script!* And he's answered by this fourth party who yells, *Who needs a script? We're doing this the good old-fashioned way!*"

"Oh, dear," said Lewis.

"You can say that again, brother," said Joseph from the bathroom, stropping his razor. "By this time, I was almost at this courtyard, all moorish tiles, with the crazy house right ahead. Just then this door in the mosque opened, see, and out came these two guys dressed in burnooses. I scrammed up some steps to one side and hid, as much as I could, which wasn't much but neither of the mortals was looking my way. One of them was saying to the other one, *Aw, come on, be a sport. It'll be fun!*

"And I thought to myself, 'Isn't that the little guy who's playing Moonshine?'"

"Otis Harlan?"

"Yeah!"

"Otis *Happy the Dwarf* Harlan?"

"Look, who else has a voice like that? But then, the other mortal guy says: *No, no, I really don't think I'd better,* and instantly I knew it was Sterling Holloway because—well, who else has a voice like *that*? He says further, *I'm sure you meant well, but I didn't know it was this kind of party. Are you sure Jack knows about this?*

"And Harlan says, *Sure he does! You should see the parties he throws here! Look, stick around. You don't have to be in the movie. I'll introduce you to Maisie. She's a swell conversationalist.*" Joseph paused to shave his upper lip.

"Movie?" said Lewis.

"But Holloway just mumbled his regrets, and Harlan lowered his voice and started in about how he hoped Holloway was going to keep his lip buttoned about all this anyhow, on account of the Hays code. This was when I decided to try to get a peek into the garden, since that seemed to be where most of the noise was coming from. So I crept up the stairs and looked over the top and—what a scene, folks, what a scene!"

"What kind of scene?"

"It was another tiled terrace, O.K.? With a reflecting pool in the middle. And right below me was a wall sloping down in a sort of a ziggurat thing, and on the wall was this huge mosaic tile picture of a spider in a web. And this girl was leaning against it, as two guys in robes were putting fake manacles on her wrists, and they were all three giggling. She was stark naked except for some costume jewelry. I was looking straight down between her breasts and right there, looking back up at me, was the Tavernier Violet.

"The whole place was lit up bright as day with studio lights. There was a big old camera, and a director's chair, across the pool, and about fifteen guys and a handful of dames, everybody dressed in Arabian Nights getup. Over to one side there was a table with a punchbowl, and a hookah, and people lined up to take their turns at gin punch or marijuana, which would explain all the giggling.

RUDE MECHANICALS

"I spotted Fletcher, and a bunch of other studio folks, Barrymore included. 'Hah,' I said to myself, 'Hah, Mr. Profile, so this is another of your hideouts! Won't Mr. Mayer be interested to learn about *this*! If Mr. Mayer doesn't have a coronary arrest first.' Right then one of the sheiks finishes his cup of hooch, strides over to the director's chair, and plants himself in it. 'Holy Smoke!' I said to myself, 'It's Harold Lloyd!'"

"No!" Lewis was scandalized. "Not *Harold Lloyd!*"

"What, you're surprised? You hadn't heard he was a photography enthusiast?"

"*The Freshman* Harold Lloyd?"

"Yeah. Him. He sat himself down and yelled, *Ready on stage, everyone!* And everybody scrambled to their marks. Lloyd said, *O.K., the Loyal Sons of the Sheik and Screw-The-Talkies Productions presents Reel Two of 'The Sins of Old Babylon'! The sacrifice of the virgin to the Spider-God! The desert nomads have worked themselves into a frenzy of lust. Doris, you don't know what to expect. You're terrified, because you know what brutes men are, right? And here you are with them feasting their eyes on your fair white body. What do you imagine they'll do next, huh? Wait a minute, she's not fastened TO anything! You bunch of idiots! Cripes! Quick, somebody, get some rope!*

"And the girl yells, *Look, youse guys, either figure out what you're doing or get me a bathrobe!*

"And Fletcher himself came running up with a bathrobe and slipped it around her while this other son of the desert brought a piece of rope. He tied one end to the chain connecting Doris's manacles and threw the other one up at the top of the ziggurat, see, right by where I was hiding, and I could see he was trying to loop it over a water pipe sticking out there. So I backed down the steps as fast as I could, while he was scrambling up and tying off the rope. By this time nobody was in the courtyard. I could hear Holloway out in the drive, trying to get his car started.

"Then I heard Lloyd yell, *O.K.! Camera!* And somebody's clapperboard shut with a *clop,* and I heard the camera cranking away. I figured it was now or never, so I ran around the side of the hill. I couldn't see so well in the damn peanut head, so I lost a few seconds stumbling around trying to find a way to the pool terrace, and finally crawled through some bushes on my hands and knees. Suddenly I came out right behind one of the big spotlights.

"There, across the pool, was Doris the Virgin Sacrifice, batting her eyelashes and miming horror at Myron the Lecherous Spider-Priest, who was making a couple of half-hearted passes at her with a big wooden scimitar. As I watched, up strode Bill the Desert Chieftain, and stuck up one arm, and said *No! We rode across many sand dunes to capture this beautiful slave! The Spider-God will not deny us our reward!* And he threw his robe open, and guess what?"

"I don't think I want to know," said Lewis.

"Yeah, well, I didn't either, but there it was for the whole world to see, and as Myron the Spider-Priest dropped his scimitar in feigned horror, guess what happened next?" Joseph slapped on after-shave.

"You mean they were shooting a pornographic film?" Lewis realized belatedly.

"So, since everybody's attention was pretty well riveted on the action, I figured I probably wouldn't get a better chance for a surprise attack. I took a running jump and cleared the pool, knocked Myron the Spider-Priest into the pool, shoved Bill the Desert Chieftain to one side, grabbed the Tavernier Violet, and ran like crazy for the far edge of the terrace. And jumped off."

"And the cameras were running the whole time?"

"Yeah. That's one stag film that'll make history. So there I was, rocketing down the hill pretty much on my back, and getting a little worried because it's quite a bit steeper than I'd thought it would be, and suddenly there's this tree coming at me. I threw myself sideways, but I swear this branch leaped out and hit my wrist."

"And you let go of the diamond," said Lewis.

"No! I had a death-grip on the damn thing, but I was clutching it by the chain. Which had broken when I yanked it off the dame's neck. And I was wearing those damn white Mickey Mouse mitts anyway, which made it harder to keep a grip. I had one of those slow-motion moments where I watched the rock go shooting away, like the chain was a whip snapping, and *katang*! It flicked out into the void of night. And dropped into the gulf of despair. And landed in the back seat of Sterling Holloway's car."

"What will you do now?"

"Do you know where the guy lives, by any chance?"

"No." Lewis rubbed his eyes. "And I'm not taking you on a desperate search, either. I've got to be at the Bowl at four this afternoon, and I haven't slept in forty-eight hours."

"Real cyborgs don't need sleep."

"This one does. Joseph, the dress rehearsal is tonight, for gods' sake."

"Dress rehearsal, huh? So Holloway's got to be there too! Keen. Now, what do you say we go get some flannel cakes at Musso and Frank's?" Joseph pulled on a clean shirt and beamed at Lewis's reflection in the mirror.

Eight

Through bog, through bush, through brake, through briar...

Lewis was still yawning as he made his way up from the Bowl parking lot, threading his way between the piers that supported the trestle. He didn't spot Joseph until he was seated beside Reinhardt, listening to the Los Angeles Philharmonic storm through Mendelssohn's Overture. Joseph was crouched on the trestle, high above the scene, installing a series of black-painted two-by-fours along the trestle's edge and connecting them with lengths of black velvet rope. He winked and gave Lewis a thumb's up.

Lewis nodded at him, briefly, and returned his attention to Reinhardt, who was watching the stage with furrowed brow. Theseus's court was hastily blocked out on the wood-land set by standards and drapery, carried by sweating little boys in Moorish blackface and turbans. Theseus took center stage and declaimed about the slowness of the old moon waning, in tones that suggested he was just dying to take Hippolyta away to Martha's Vineyard for a post-nuptial bottle of bubbly.

The next scene, with the rival suitors, went badly. Olivia de Havilland was fiery and charming as Hermia, but neither Lysander nor Demetrius seemed to comprehend the meaning of their lines. Helena, entering late, had a good grasp of the role but couldn't project or make her gestures wide enough to suit Reinhardt. At his insistence, she spoke her entire soliloquy four times in succession, and by the end truly sounded despairing and heartsick.

Enter the clowns. Most of them, anyway.

"Wo ist Mondshein?" muttered Reinhardt, peering at the stage.

There's Holloway! Joseph transmitted. *I'll go ransack his car!* Lewis glanced up to see Joseph scrambling down the side of the trestle upside down, which so unnerved him that he stammered as he translated Reinhardt's question. The assistant director glared at the other comedians.

"He was just driving up as we went on," said Reicher, attempting to soothe Weissberger.

"Here I am!" Harlan came bustling onstage, out of breath but grinning. "Sorry, folks!" He took his place and elbowed Holloway, adding *sotto voce,* "You missed a swell party, and how!"

Their scene proceeded. Bottom, played by Connolly as a slightly pompous know-it-all, was just displaying his prowess in roaring as gently as any sucking dove, when a distinctly ungentle roar cut through the ether to Lewis.

WHERE IS IT???

Lewis flinched. Miss Sibley, seated behind him, leaned forward and put her hand on his shoulder.

"Are you all right, Mr. Kensington?"

Lewis nodded and waved his hand dismissively. "Just a little headache," he whispered, but braced himself.

THE GODDAM THING ISN'T HERE!

Are you sure it fell in the car? It didn't bounce out again? Perhaps you ought to go look in the bushes along Pacific View—

No. I saw it land! It fell in his sheik costume. He'd taken the robe off and thrown it on the floor of the back seat.

Is the robe there still?

No!

Then, I suppose he found it when he took the robe out.

Maybe. Why me? Oh, by all the frick-frackin' gods, why me? What would you do if you found a big purple diamond while you were getting rid of the evidence of a really embarrassing party?

Assume it had got there by mistake somehow? Stick it in my pocket?

Maybe. Yeah. Where's Holloway's pants?

In the changing tent? Lewis glanced involuntarily at the row of Army Surplus pavilions that had been set up as temporary costume and prop sheds. *But you can't go in there—*

Oh, I can't, can't I?

Lewis shivered and crossed his fingers, trying to concentrate on the rehearsal. They had made it as far as the Wood Near Athens now, Apollo be thanked. There was no more than a half hour to go until sunset. The sun had already fallen behind the high ridge to the west, though it still lit the face of Mount Hollywood with red slanting light. The Bowl valley had filled up with clear blue twilight, that had been unobtrusively deepening; now the electrician hit a switch. Winking fireflies lit up the forest on the stage.

One minor effect, and suddenly it all came together. The green gloom of the forest was haunted, living and breathing, a door into an eternal summer night. Lewis heard Miss Sibley catch her breath, clap her hands. He saw Reinhardt's shoulders relax a little.

"You see?" Reinhardt said quietly. "We always come back to this place."

The musicians had to be cued twice, but reprised the overture and set the scene. The shadows deepened. The principal danseuse flitted onstage in gauzy rags, a moth in the night; Puck emerged from the branches, the most disturbing little snub-nosed monster it would be possible to meet in a dark country lane, and shrieked his opening lines…

Lewis, I'm in a jam.

The spell broke. Lewis transmitted in real irritation: *Well, get yourself out of it!*

No, seriously.

You can't get into the changing tent, can you?

I did, actually. Crawled in under the back. I'm there now. Hiding behind the clothes rack. Just finished looking through Holloway's street clothes.

Well, was the diamond in his pocket?

No. That's not the problem, though. What the hell are all these greyhounds for?

What?

There are, like, six greyhounds tethered outside the tent door. They can tell I'm in here.

They're the hounds for Theseus' entrance in Act Four. You know: "My hounds are bred out of the Spartan kind/ So flew'd, so sanded—"

Lewis, never mind the damn—Huh? Shouldn't they be beagles, then?

You'd think so, but—

I could outrun a beagle, easy. Well, so what are the chances you can come down here and get the dog handler to take 'em for a walk, or something? They're, uh, starting to growl.

Why don't you simply crawl out the way you came?

Because there's some mortal standing behind the tent now, having a smoke. Besides, I think I know—HOLY MACKEREL!

Lewis shifted in his seat, listening for the baying of ravening greyhounds. He heard none, however; and, after a moment, ventured to transmit.

Are you still there, Joseph?

Yeah.

What's happening?

I'm looking at the Tavernier Violet.

Oh, good. Can I get back to my own mission, now?

I don't have it; I'm just looking at it. It's in a big fancy hat, on a wig head on the makeup table on the ladies' side of the tent. There's a couple mortal hairdressers sitting right next to it, gossiping. I just heard one of them say, 'Wasn't that nice of Mr. Holloway, donating that piece of costume jewelery he found?' And the other one said, 'It's such a perfect accent to the costume, too.' See, the hat's all purple and gold.

Well then, why don't you grab it and run?

The goddam dogs are still outside. I'll just wait here. Sooner or later they'll step out for a break, right? Then I'll grab it. And, believe me, once it's in my hands, no mortal is going to be able to pry it out of my grip. I'll exit through the roof if I have to.

Good for you. I will now return to my regular programming.

Oh, ha ha.

Lewis relaxed and watched the play. Fairies pirouetted on the greensward, all silver and cellophane, leading the little mortal child round and round. Now came the dark host, goblins beckoning to entice him away to Oberon's court. Now the clash between moonlight and shadow, the unearthly custody quarrel. *This* part worked; Shakespeare's images, freed from print and grammar and the wooden incomprehension of the actors. Every mortal child knew there were things that fluttered and squeaked in the moonlight, and things that lurked in darkness where the trees came down to the fence line, and that it was perilous to venture out to play with them…Lewis felt a primal shiver.

Out came one pair of mortal lovers, and Lysander at least spoke with iron tongue. Reinhardt, listening, groaned quietly and shook his head. He got up and walked to the edge of the apron, signaling for the assistant director, and Lewis scrambled after him. Together, the three of them spent a fruitless five minutes trying to convey a sense of motivation to the young man, and finally retired to let Art take its course.

Lewis was murmuring a quiet prayer to the Muse Thalia when he picked up the growing crackle of Joseph's impatience.

Still down there, are you?

The clowns just left. Before that, one of the costume ladies was reading aloud from the latest issue of Silver Screen. *Helen Hayes' tips on making a marriage work. Don't any of these mortals ever need to use the bathroom, for crying out loud?*

How does Helen Hayes make her marriage work?

How should I know? I wasn't paying attention.

Lewis tuned him out and focused on the play. More lovers, more moonlight, more magic and misunderstanding. Where the actors were equal to their lines, or where the stagecraft carried it, things spun along beautifully; but there were some dismal halts.

Reinhardt began running his hands through his hair in agitation. He went onstage and remained there, with Lewis obliged to follow at his heel. He worked painfully through the staging of the four-way lovers' quarrel, with its overlapping dialogue ending in screams. Nor was he able to relax in the scenes between Bottom and Titania, for the ass's head had to be removed and refitted twice before Connolly was able to make his lines understood.

Great! The dogs have just been led away!

Good gods, are you still down there? Lewis had forgotten about Joseph.

Where else would I go? I'm going to grab the rock and run for it, Lewis—oh, crap. Here come a bunch of fairies and human bats. Jeez, there must be fifty extras lining up to change costumes. Isn't the damn play almost over?

There's still the torchlight procession to the Wedding March.

Oh, fine.

Puck got the magic flower business right at last, the mismatched lovers re-matched, and Theseus and Hippolyta came on with dogs and attendants to wake them. Bottom returned to his mates. A Happy Ending was decreed. There was a burst of subvocal cursing from the direction of the direction of the costume tent.

What's the trouble now?

The dame! Hippolyta! She's just had the headdress put on! No!

It's her costume for the Wedding Procession, Joseph.

No! There she goes! I'll never reach her, through this crowd! Where are they all going?

Up on the hill for the procession.

Up the hill, huh? In the dark? Hmmm.

Joseph, what are you going to do?

See you later, Lewis.

Wait! What—

Lewis heard a shrill scream from the direction of the costume tent, even as the crowd of actors straggled to the edge of the Bowl valley. He peered into the darkness beyond the lit stage, but saw only fathomless blackness until he switched to infrared. The night became a spectral green, through which the mortals walked in glowing scarlet silhouette. The men wore tights and tunics in a vaguely medieval-Venetian style, with immense bicorn hats like fans;

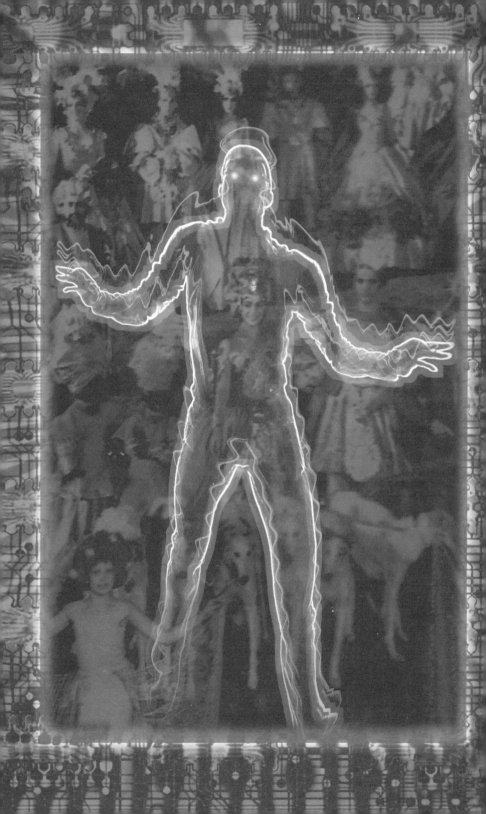

the ladies wore hoop skirts with panniers, great unwieldy affairs, and tall headdresses of ostrich plumes. They reached the foot of the hill and one or two thoughtful ones switched on flashlights, looking for a path up.

There wasn't one. Lewis heard clearly the muttered complaints, and then the beam of someone's flashlight picked out the small flag Reinhardt had had planted, on the crest of the hill, to mark their starting point.

"We have to get up *there*? This is ridiculous!"

"It isn't as steep as it looks, Mr. Lodge—"

"There is a trail here, somewhere—" Lewis recognized the voice of the assistant director. "Professor Reinhardt chose this spot carefully—the whole audience must be able to see you from their seats, you understand—"

"But in these costumes?"

"May I remind you this is Dress Rehearsal?"

"Somebody light one of the torches!"

"No! On your cue, if you please—Here, follow me—"

The great pulsing scarlet crowd began to seep uphill in a tentative sort of way, with a thread of mortals scrambling through the brush. And…flanking them to the right was a skulking figure in blue-green, flickering with other colors as he stalked them.

Joseph, what are you doing?

I'm going to get the damn diamond. Whatever it takes.

But you can't—

Reinhardt, who had been making his way up from the stage, sat down beside Lewis and looked at his watch.

"I'm afraid they're a little late stepping off, Herr Professor," Lewis stammered. Reinhardt shrugged.

"This is why one has rehearsals," he said. Lewis looked back at the hillside. The mortals were nearly at the top of the ridge now, in a throng that glowed like a bed of live coals.

The bluegreen figure could just be glimpsed some little distance down the ridge, advancing on them stealthily. It ran a few steps—halted—dodged around a bush and gained a few more yards. It was remarkably like watching wildlife footage of a wolf stalking a herd of sheep. Lewis felt an irrational urge to shout in warning.

The mortals wouldn't have heard him, though…

"Is everybody here?"

"Where are the torches? Not the electric torches, you idiot!"

"Mr. Weissberger, I can't see a thing—"

"Mr. Weissberger, I lost one of my slippers, I've got to go back and look for it—"

"Everyone, please, form up! Mr. Lodge, Signorina Braggiotti, this is your mark, here by the flag—will the rest of you please—"

"Mr. Weissberger, there's no path marked out—"

"We will simply walk downhill to the foot of the ramp," shouted Weissberger, rather V-ing his Ws in his stress. "It will not be a difficulty! Clyde, we will now distribute the torches!"

Beside Lewis, Reinhardt checked his watch again. Lewis bit his lower lip, watching as one unwary mortal strayed from the flock, going back down the way he had come. Looking for a lost slipper? Yes. He crouched, picked up something and balanced unsteadily on one foot as he pulled it on.

Oh, foolish mortal; for here came the bluegreen figure, slipping up behind the scarlet one. Bop! Lewis winced, as the scarlet figure collapsed and was dragged into a thicket. Colors shifted and flashed from within the thicket, and then the bluegreen figure emerged, having appropriated the mortal's costume. Absurd hat slightly askew, it scrambled up the hill to the end of the line that had formed, and grabbed a torch.

"The torches have now been distributed!" Weissberger's voice cracked. "On my signal, the torches will be lowered! Now!"

A figure at the front of the line suddenly glowed with a point of white heat. Squinting, Lewis made out the propmaster, who had lit a cigar.

"The torches will now be lit!" screamed Weissberger. The propmaster puffed his cigar to brightness and went hurriedly along the line of torches, dabbing its lit end on each of them in turn. One by one they flared alight. There was scattered applause from the benches all around Lewis. Reinhardt merely nodded in satisfaction.

"AND NOW!" Weissberger turned and spoke through a megaphone. "HERR PROFESSOR, WE ARE READY!"

Reinhardt waved his arms for the benefit of the conductor, who turned and raised his baton. The trumpet players sounded the fanfare, and the whole orchestra sailed into Mendelssohn's *Wedding March*.

The procession stepped off. The long line of torches moved uncertainly through the night, with the assistant director and stage manager scuttling ahead through the sagebrush with flashlights, searching for a trail. Lewis watched the bluegreen figure at the end of the line craning its neck, studying the mortals ahead of it. It lowered its torch, crept off to one side, and then a stentorian voice called:

"Jeepers, look out! That's a rattlesnake!"

There were screams of alarm from the hillside. Torches wavered wildly, one or two were dropped and hastily retrieved, a bush caught fire and had to be beaten out. One actress, leaping out of the way of any reptile threat, overbalanced and fell backward into a spurge laurel. Her hoops collapsed around her like a Japanese lantern folding up, and her frantic legs were white-hot as they kicked the air, rapidly cooling to red. She had to be hauled upright by a pair of her fellow extras. Weissberger came charging back up the slope, ready to club any snakes he found with his flashlight, and vainly beat the bushes for a moment or two.

"What is happening?" Reinhardt stood, scowling. He shielded his eyes with his hand and peered out across the valley. Miss Sibley handed him a megaphone. "WEISS-BERGER, WHY HAVE THEY STOPPED?" he bellowed, over the orchestra.

The assistant director went scrambling back, grabbed his megaphone from the propmaster, and called back: "IT WAS A SNAKE!"

"WAS ANYONE BITTEN?"

"NEIN, HERR PROFESSOR!"

"THEN PLEASE PROCEED!"

Weissberger turned and made desperate shooing motions at the milling actors. Altogether it was five minutes before the wavering line re-formed, and when it did, Lewis saw that the bluegreen figure had managed to advance halfway up the line of the procession.

By this time, however, the *Wedding March* had ended. The conductor turned and looked up at Reinhardt inquiringly.

"Play it again," said Reinhardt, forgetting to use the megaphone. Lewis waved his arms, semaphoring an encore. Once again the fanfare sounded, and once again the procession stepped off.

Dum dum dah *dum*dum *dum*dum *dah* diddly-*dah* diddly-*dah*—

The line of torches advanced in a tentative kind of way, bobbing along through the dark.

"Oh, my God, that's a coyote! And it's rabid! Run, everybody!"

There was immediate chaos on the hillside. Lewis saw the bluegreen figure dart out of line again, questing forward, but it collided and went down in a tangle of panicked mortals. There was a wild confusion of arms, legs, plumes, hoops and floppy hats. Some mortal gave an agonized yell.

"It bit me! Help! It bit me on the leg!"

"Where did it go?"

"There it is! You can see its glowing eyes!"

"I heard it growling!"

"Did it break the skin?"

"We must be near its den or something!"

"Hit it with a torch! They're afraid of fire!"

"Where is it?"

"Stop this at once! You will resume the line of march!"

"Listen, we were just attacked by a wild animal!"

"What? Where?"

"There it is! Shine your damn flashlight in that bush!"

A second of silence.

"Well? Where is it?"

"Well—well—it was crouching right there, a second ago!"

"I saw it too!"

"This is mass hysteria. Get into line, you idiots!"

"Say, do you want a punch in the mouth?"

"You can't talk that way to Americans!"

"You call yourselves actors? You will be fired!"

Someone took a swing at someone else, who dodged, but the blow kept coming and hit a third party, who dropped his torch and hit back, and another person was cracked across the shins with a flashlight, and it only got worse from there. Lewis cringed.

"They have stopped again," observed Reinhardt.

"Yes, I'm afraid they have," said Lewis.

"Why is this?" Reinhardt stood up and raised the megaphone. "IF YOU PLEASE! LET US CONTINUE!"

The orchestra faltered to a stop. Lewis saw the seething mass of pugilism halt, as though coming to its senses, and then grudgingly re-form the processional line. A couple of torches had to be re-lit. Several hats had to be located.

"WEISSBERGER?"

"THERE HAS BEEN A MOMENTARY DELAY!"

"WELL, WE WILL BEGIN THE MARCH AGAIN!"

"JAWOHL, HERR PROFES—WHAT DID YOU JUST CALL ME?"

The fanfare sounded yet again, and perhaps prevented further bloodshed, for the sullen line jolted forward and then, miraculously, kept on coming through the darkness. They were nearly over the last rise before the foot of the trestle now. Lewis, unable to look away, saw the bluegreen figure fall out and run slinking along the side, shoving to get further ahead. Further now still, ever closer to the front of the line where walked the tall stately figures of Theseus and Hippolyta, up until this point relatively untouched by the general mayhem.

"Hey! Who's pushing?"

"Stop that!"

"Well, aren't you the rude—"

"Say, what do you think you're doing?"

Here came the procession, onto the trestle at last: first Weissberger walking backwards (the propmaster had prudently decided to fall out and cross the parking lot underneath), one hand on the velvet rope to guide himself. Next came Theseus and Hippolyta, Mr. Lodge and Ms. Braggiotti, and now Lewis could make out the sparkle of their jewels—and, yes, there was the familiar glint of the

Tavernier Violet, square in the center of Hippolyta's gold lamé turban.

They had come into the range of the spotlights at last and Lewis switched from infrared vision, but not before he caught a glimpse of the bluegreen figure hurtling forward through the line. The other members of the procession staggered and nearly fell, several dropped their torches over the side—they streamed down through the night like flaming comets—and there were more cries of anger and alarm.

What—no, you can't, not here! Lewis jumped to his feet involuntarily. Reinhardt turned his head to stare at Lewis and so missed seeing the bedraggled figure that thrust its way past the blackamoors holding Hippolyta's train. On it came, and Weissberger saw it now and raised his flashlight threateningly.

"You will get back to your appointed place!" he said.

Joseph dodged a blow from the flashlight, sprang upward, ripped the Tavernier Violet from Hippolyta's headdress, and narrowly missed having Theseus' scepter broken over his head by somersaulting off the edge of the trestle. Miss Braggiotti screamed and clutched at her head. Lewis bit his knuckles. He saw Joseph catch a beam halfway down and swing himself, apelike, to the inner framework, where he clambered to the ground and ran.

"What was that?" Reinhardt rose to his feet. "Are there monkeys in California?"

"Perhaps one escaped from a circus," said Lewis, for lack of anything better to say. The procession, thank all the gods, had recovered itself, and here came Weissberger down the ramp with his flashlight, grimly determined to lead them to the stage. Hippolyta's headdress was slightly askew, and missing its violet centerpiece, but she was otherwise unharmed. Lewis sank into his seat, vastly relieved.

As the final crashing chords of the *Wedding March* sounded, the procession stepped forth on stage and hit their respective marks.

"*Gott sei dank,*" murmured Reinhardt. Lodge faced front and declaimed:

"What the hell is going on? Miss Braggiotti was just assaulted!"

"It was some lunatic, masquerading as an actor," said Weissberger, who had seen the whole thing. "Please, madam, calm yourself. He probably just wanted an autograph. We will have him arrested if he comes near you again. And now, if you please, Herr Lodge, your line?"

Lodge harrumphed, but struck an attitude and began:

"Come now; what masques, what dances shall we have
To wear away this long age of three hours—"

"Hey!" Moonshine made an early entrance, waving his arms. "Hey, somebody's car is on fire back there!"

*"Between our after-supper and bed-time—*I beg your pardon?"

"What did he say?" Reinhardt asked, but an ominous red glow from beneath the trestle was making it plain now.

"One of you guys dropped a torch and it rolled under somebody's car!"

"Someone call the fire department!"

"Get the fire buckets!"

"It's not my car, is it?" John Lodge ran to the crowd that had assembled at the edge of the stage, peering vainly back at the conflagration.

No, thought Lewis, in sad resignation. *I'll just bet I know whose car it is.*

The fire engines had departed by the time Lewis made his weary way down Highland Avenue on foot. As he passed the American Legion Hall, a disheveled figure emerged from the bushes and fell into step beside him.

"Say...sorry about your car, Lewis."

Lewis considered socking him, and decided against it. He'd only drop Reinhardt's promptbook, and undoubtedly miss Joseph in any case.

Nine

Will it please you to see the epilogue…?

Lewis adjusted the fit of his tuxedo jacket and frowned at himself in the mirror. However nicely his suits draped at the tailor's, by the time he put them on they always seemed to have expanded a size. He got out an old-fashioned leather hatbox, opened it, and drew out his black silk top hat. It was a veteran of opening nights going back as far as *Chu Chin Chow*, but still looked as smart as when he'd bought it in Oxford Street. Anything lasted, if you took proper care of it.

And what if he was reluctant to let go of things, especially memories? Memories were all an immortal could truly call his own. In the end, whatever the end might be, they were all he would have.

He set the hat on his head and tilted it back at a jaunty angle. All he needed now was a walking stick.

On his way to the umbrella stand, his glance fell on the promptbook. Reinhardt had taken Lewis's meticulously-faked copy, and slipped it into his briefcase without so much as a second glance. Lewis would deliver the original to the Company's shipping depot in the morning, but for now…best to be cautious. He scooped it up in one hand, and with the other took down the framed print of *Love Among the Ruins* that concealed his wall safe. Having secured the promptbook, he re-hung the print, looked at it wistfully a moment, and turned away. Time to go; he had a long walk to the Bowl.

As he stepped out on the sidewalk, however, Joseph's Ford came around the corner. Its left front fender was now green, its door was blue, and the left rear fender was a sort of a rust color. Joseph hit the horn twice, and threw Lewis a centurion's salute, grinning.

"Hey, Lewis, want a ride?"

"How thoughtful of you!" Lewis opened the door. Joseph reached over and swept a pair of tennis shoes and an empty Nehi bottle from the seat so he could get in.

"Hey, it's the least I could do, pal." He wore a suit that was clean and freshly pressed, if not exactly evening attire.

"Where's the Tavernier Violet?"

"In a pair of long johns at the back of my sock drawer," said Joseph. "Completely safe." He looked Lewis over and whistled. "Boy, you're dressed to kill! I didn't think people wore white tie and tails unless they could afford box seats, nowadays."

Lewis pulled out the pair of tickets he'd been given. "Section D, Row 9, Seats 14 and 16," he read aloud. "It's still an evening at the theater. One likes to uphold a certain standard, after all."

"Gotta change with the times, though, Lewis," said Joseph. He pulled away from the curb and stepped on the gas. "Otherwise, the mortals notice."

They left the Ford in the lower parking lot and made their way through the mortal crowds. The trestle bridge still stood, only slightly scorched in one area; the charred wreck of Lewis's car had been hauled away, and in its place a battery of klieg lights raked at the evening sky, sending white beams sweeping across.

Flashbulbs burst like actinic bubbles: Lewis turned his face to the cameras and glimpsed Reinhardt, posing in a tuxedo with Miss Sibley and the editor of the *Los Angeles Times*. Reporters were shouting questions in English, which Miss Sibley was answering.

Reinhardt was smiling, uneasy and uncomprehending. Looking at his eyes, Lewis knew he had already withdrawn from the alien soil, in fact from the mortal world, and was walking in spirit under the haunted trees. The Reichstag had burned, old Hindenburg was dead, and a petty politician whom no one had ever taken seriously had used fear to bully his democratic nation into a dictatorship, almost overnight. None of it made any sense. And Reinhardt was stranded here, in this crazy place, and could never go home again. Who wouldn't retreat into the Wood Near Athens?…

Lewis sighed. Joseph jostled his arm.

"Hey, there's a guy selling programs. You want one?"

The benches were wood weathered to silver, pale as marble in the lights, and rose in a semicircle like the marble seats in any theater in the classical world. The night air was Mediterranean-warm, smelled of pine trees, aromatic brush on the hills. You might almost imagine you were in Athens, if you closed your eyes; but only almost. The voices were all wrong.

Lewis opened his eyes, distracted by the mortal chatter of Southern California's cultural elite. Down in the boxes he saw furs and pearls, opera glasses, a few silk hats like his own; higher up, in the tiers that rose to the back of the house, were the people who had taken the streetcars to get here, who munched popcorn as they waited for the spectacle, or took stealthy nips of gin from pocket flasks. Most of them had never seen a Shakespeare play in their lives. What would they make of tonight's entertainment? Reinhardt's transplanted forest seemed dwarfed by the staggering towers of light from the klieg lamps, small and unreal, nearly transparent.

It got worse when the president of the California Festival Association came out to make a speech, going on at some length about the forward-looking citizens of California who, in partnership with the California State Chamber of Commerce, deeply and spiritually yearned to establish California in her rightful place as one of the leaders of the cultural and artistic world. Joseph chuckled and nudged Lewis.

"If only they knew," he said.

The lights went down at last. For a long moment there was only starlight, for the three-quarter moon had not yet risen above the hill to the east. Lewis crossed his fingers. *Click!* The fireflies lit, and a couple of carefully-concealed can lights. There was the forest! Suddenly the trees were immense and ancient, suddenly the real world faded away and the dream was palpable. From the audience all around him Lewis heard the indrawn breath, one universal *oooh* of delight. He relaxed, leaning back.

All in all, it was a pleasant experience, though the painful parts were uncommonly painful. The lesser actors recited their lines with such flat lack of understanding they might have been reading from a Sears and Roebuck catalogue. The fairies twittered, Oberon overacted, Titania was shrill.

The mortals, however, didn't notice. Reinhardt's spell had worked, as effectively as the juice of the magic flower casting its glamour on the lovers' eyes. The two immortals looked around them, at the rapt audience. Joseph grinned and shrugged.

The wedding procession stepped off on cue, torches alight, and hit the stage squarely as the Wedding March ended. A bit of purple glass sparkled in Hippolyta's turban. Somewhere backstage, Felix Weissberger soaked his blistered hands in cold water and reflected that an afternoon's frenzied brush-cutting with a machete, marking out a path thereafter with clothesline, had been worth it.

Puck stood forth at last, smiling and untrustworthy.

"If we shadows have offended,
Think but this, and all is mended,
That you have but slumber'd here
While these visions did appear.
And this weak and idle theme,
No more yielding but a dream,
Gentles, do not reprehend:
If you pardon, we will mend.
Else the Puck a liar call.
So, good night unto you all.
Give me your hands, if we be friends,
And Robin shall restore amends."

Note-perfect. He bowed, scampered away into the trees, and the orchestra played Mendelssohn's closing music. The last four chords sounded; faded. The forest went dark.

The house lights came up abruptly, and Greater Los Angeles sat blinking on the benches. This was the moment when movie-goers looked around for their hats and coats and brushed off spilled popcorn. That was what the audience did now, in deafening silence. And more silence. The moment dragged out interminably.

"Oh, for crying out loud," said Joseph in disgust. "'GIVE ME YOUR HANDS, IF WE BE FRIENDS!'"

He began to applaud, and Lewis joined in, and the gentry down in the boxes collected their wits and applauded too. The rest of the audience, those at least who were not already streaming for the exits in anticipation of a massive traffic jam in the Cahuenga Pass and Red Cars packed like sardine cans, finally realized that perhaps a sign of their appreciation was in order. There was some scattered applause.

Joseph and Lewis stayed in their seats until the crowd had ebbed away, as those few sensible locals did, and then strolled down at their leisure. Lewis glanced out at the Wood near Athens, which had once again retreated into unreality. There was Max Reinhardt on the stage, shoulders sagging, staring up at the empty seats in dismay.

"Wait a minute," he told Joseph. He made his way through the boxes to the edge of the orchestra pit, and took off his hat.

"Herr Professor?"

Reinhardt turned his head. He looked as though he vaguely recognized Lewis.

"They really did enjoy it, you know. They're just not used to live theater."

"You think so?" Reinhardt's air of despondency did not lift.

"Wait till you see the morning papers! It'll be a smash hit. They'll have to add extra performances," promised Lewis.

"And how would you know that, young man?"

"Because you're a genius," said Lewis.

"Is America a good place in which to be a genius?"

"Well, of course it is."

Reinhardt looked out into the black void of Hollywood. "I hope so," he said bleakly.

Ten

But come, your Bergomask; let your epilogue alone.

"Duh I entice yuh? Duh I speak yuh fair? Or rather duh I not in plainest truth tell yuh I duh not nor I cannot act?" recited Lewis in a monotone. Joseph snickered.

They were seated in a booth in Musso and Frank's, enjoying a late supper. Though it was near midnight, the place was crowded with the nocturnal denizens of show business: producers making pitches to studio executives, directors making pitches to producers, agents making pitches to directors, and actors begging their agents for work. Here and there a writer, lonely as a leper, sat brooding under the forest mural, over a fourth or fifth drink.

"I thought it was pretty neat, bad acting and all," said Joseph, loosening his tie. "Too bad the movie's going to be such a flopperola. Just as well Reinhardt can't know that in advance."

"People will still be watching it in a century's time," said Lewis. "I wish I could have told him that, at least."

Joseph shook his head. "You were pushing it, telling him as much as you did. You know the rules. Would they be able to handle it, if they knew as much as we do about the future? Hell no. *'Lord, what fools these mortals be.'*"

"They aren't the only ones," said Lewis ruefully. A waiter appeared out of the shadows, bearing their cocktails on a tray. "Ah! And a perfect martini appeared, as if by magic. Thank you, Manuel."

The waiter withdrew. Joseph raised his scotch and soda. "Here's to absent friends."

"Oh, gosh, if we drink to absent friends we'll be here all night," said Lewis.

"Good point. What'll we drink to, then? The rise of the Arts in Southern California? A bullet for Hitler? Good old Will Shakespeare?"

"To Max Reinhardt," said Lewis.

"There you go," said Joseph, and drank.

"'*And so good night unto you all,*'" said Lewis. He raised his martini. It caught the light from the booth lamp and shimmered frostily, bright as the moon's silver visage on a landscape of ephemeral sleep.